No One Lives Forever

By
Robert Fisher

La Maison

La Maison Publishing, Inc.
Vero Beach, Florida
The Hibiscus City
lamaisonpublishing@gmail.com

Table of Contents

Chapter 1 ....

Alley Side Reflection 1

Chapter 2 ....

Pulling Weeds 8

Chapter 3 ....

They 14

Chapter 4 ....

Stay the Hand 21

Chapter 5 ....

Moonlight over Spy City 33

Chapter 6 ....

The Athenian Connection 42

Chapter 7 ....

Means To An End 57

Chapter 8 ....

A Take It Or Leave It Type Deal 66

Chapter 9 ....

.22 Caliber Princess 81

Chapter 10 ....

The Cobalt Express 95

Chapter 11...

Through Hells Creation 106

Chapter 12...

Pieces On A Chessboard...................................115

Chapter 13...

Sunset Riders...122

Chapter 14...

Wacky Racers 129

Chapter 15...

Riders On The Storm 137

Chapter 16...

The Mad Max Fan Club 142

Chapter 17...

Hitting the Fan 150

Chapter 18...

Brick In The Wall 158

Chapter 19...

The House Of Stone 166

Chapter 20...

The Dancing Puppets 172

Chapter 21...

Face Of The Enemy 181

Chapter 22 ....

Damage Control.. 188

Chapter 23 ....

Money To Burn 195

Chapter 24 ....

The Glittering Kingdom... 202

Chapter 25 ....

Million Dollar Rundown... 208

Chapter 26 ....

Return to the Black Kingdom................................. 215

Chapter 1
Alley Side Reflection

The sun above rained oppressive waves of heat on the Moroccan city of Tangier. During his time as a Silhouette agent, Simon Kane had been to Tangier multiple times and the oppressive heat of the coastal desert metropolis never changed once. Simon stood leaning against the door of the car parked in the dingy alley. Across the street was the shelter where Mai was working. Simon wiped the sweat from his brow, silently cursing himself for wearing his dark blue trench coat. Though he hated to admit it he needed the trench coat on since it covered his gun and the last thing they needed was to get arrested.

Ordinarily he'd be in the shelter guarding Mai but she told him to wait outside since the eye patch covering the remains of his right eye tended to frighten some of the children in the shelter. He briefly considered getting back in the car and turning on the AC for some relief but decided against it since being inside the car would limit his vision. He checked his watch to see how long Mai had been inside, he sighed impatiently at seeing that he had been waiting for her for the last thirty minutes. Down the street was a small restaurant selling bocadillos, a Spanish delicacy consisting of chicken on a baguette roll with tomatoes, onions and other toppings. Simon thought about buying one to eat while waiting for Mai but decided to wait till dinner.

In an effort to take his mind off his hunger, Simon shifted his attention to his surroundings. The alley was located in one of the more unsavory parts of Tangier, but as unsavory as it was, he had seen worse.

It had been a unique odyssey these last few months thought Simon. He was a former agent of the CIA's elite black ops unit codenamed

Silhouette. He, his wife and a fellow agent were reenlisted by Silhouette to investigate a weapons theft. They tracked the theft to Belarus where his wife was killed by Counselor Black, an agent of a mysterious criminal organization known as the Networc. Three months later he was hired by the leader of the Heise She Li Triad to rescue his daughter, Mai Yunao, from the Rojas Cartel on Sankan Island. In exchange, the Triad would assemble a team to help him destroy their mutual enemy: The Networc. While they were assembling the team over the last five months, Simon agreed to act as Mai's bodyguard while she traveled the world working for multiple charities. If they couldn't assemble the team after six months, then the deal was off. It had been five months since they had made the deal and two weeks since he last heard from the man the Triad ordered to assemble the team, a man named Deng.

While Mai was working in South America, Deng had introduced him to one member of the team, an ex-IRA assassin turned catholic nun named Siobhan Costello. Yet he hadn't been contacted about the fourth and final member, an individual Deng referred to only as MAGIC 44, much to Simons annoyance. After Mai had finished her work in South America they went to Tangier where she had been working at a refugee shelter.

"What a long strange trip it's been," muttered Simon.

Despite his mission with Silhouette, his recruitment by the Triad and subsequent travels with Mai the same questions continued to gnaw at him. All of those questions involved the source of all of this: The Networc. From what Simon had seen and heard they had access to state-of-the-art-military technology, resources and a seemingly limitless reach and influence. So how could the Networc seemingly disappear like they did after what happened in Belarus and Sankan? It simply didn't make any sense, especially to Simon given his history. During his time with Silhouette he had encountered and shut down multiple terrorist and criminal organizations and had never heard of them, which was baffling considering Silhouettes reach.

There was another question that was even more disconcerting: what are they planning now? Simon knew all too well what they were capable of. If it weren't for Simon and his fellow Silhouette agents, the Networc would have successfully stolen nuclear weapons from Belarus six months ago for reasons he shuddered to think of. Then again, his wife and fellow Silhouette agent, Sheila Goodbody would still be alive. He shivered as the image of her getting shot in front of him by Counselor Black reverberated throughout his mind. He vowed to never let that happen to someone he cared about again.

"Hey Simon!" yelled Mai cheerfully as she opened the door of the shelter and walked toward him.

Instinctively, Simon scanned the rooftops then looked at her with a smile and a wave, grateful for the distraction. Mai Yunao was in her early twenties while Simon was in his mid-thirties. She was also the daughter of Lin Yunao, the head of the Heise She Li Triad. After their experience on Sankan and subsequent travels Simon and Mai had developed a close bond between them. Mai was a short, attractive Chinese woman with long black hair and a nerdy yet sunny disposition.

She was wearing a buttoned shirt with her glasses dangling precariously from the collar and blue jeans. "Aren't you hot in that get up," she asked as she put on her glasses.

"Nah, so how'd it go in there?" asked Simon welcoming the distraction from his ruminations on the Networc.

"Good, we helped a lot of people and I've wired them some money to keep the shelter going," she answered.

"Lord knows they need it, so where to now?" he asked.

"The hotel, I need some rest," said Mai warily. Simon was glad to hear it since it meant getting out of the heat.

"Good, I'll drive," said Simon as he opened the driver side door of the car and got in.

As Mai sat down next to him, she caught a glimpse of Simon's pistol hanging in its holster. "I wish you didn't need to carry that with you" she said regretfully as Simon started the car.

"Me neither, still would you prefer this?" replied Simon as he flicked his wrist back and from out of it popped out a small knife from his wristband, a gift from Deng and the Triad.

Mai looked at it with disapproval. "Not really."

Simon grinned as he gently pushed the knife back into its catch. As they pulled out of the alley Simon glanced up at the sky and briefly asked himself the same question: *what's going on out there?*

Chapter 2
Pulling Weeds

Abner Cohen sat in his rental car waiting for the phone call giving him the go ahead to proceed. Outside the rain came down in a never-ending barrage. "Of all the places they could hide, it had to be Berlin," he muttered. His phone rang interrupting his thoughts. The screen said Unknown caller which meant the caller was most likely his boss, Director Yossi calling from Tel Aviv.

"Yes?" he answered.

"Sitrep, agent HOPLITE," said the scrambled voice that referred to him by his codename.

Abner glanced up at his targets apartment to see if the lights were on. "Targets are in position, please advise."

After almost a full minute of waiting he got his response. "Roger that HOPLITE, proceed with Operation: NITPICK," said Director Yossi, before hanging up.

"About time," grunted Abner as he returned the phone to his pocket. He reached into his glove compartment and pressed a hidden button causing a tray to pop out from under the glove compartment. In the tray was Abner's personal sidearm, a Browning Hi-Power, next to it were two magazines and a silencer. Casually, he removed the gun and screwed on the silencer, finally he put in a fresh magazine of 9mm rounds. He placed the gun into the interior pocket of his black, raincoat. He checked to see if his black balaclava was in his pants pocket, it was.

He stepped out of the car and walked across the street and into the apartment. The lobby was empty, which was not surprising given the lateness of the hour. Abner couldn't help but feel satisfied as he entered the elevator and selected the floor he wanted.

After three months of hard work he had tracked down the terrorist cell belonging to the Nazi terrorist organization: Aquarius. He felt proud in a way to be destroying the enemies of his homeland and his people.

But he shrugged at the sad fact that for every one of them he killed more would pop up in their place like a weed. The elevator arrived at the floor, the doors opened, and Abner was looking down an empty hallway lined with doors. His targets were in a room at the end of the hall. Abner silently walked down the hall to the room. He wished he had his Galil with him, but he brushed the thought aside. When he approached the door, he looked up and down the hall to make sure he was alone.

He pulled his balaclava and black gloves out of his pocket and put them on. He grinned at the irony that he was wearing the same headgear as Black September wore during their attack on the Olympics in Munich decades ago. In addition to that, he was not only in the same country where those attacks had happened but that had once tried to exterminate his people. The irony was hard to ignore thought Abner as he pulled out his pistol and cocked it. He took a deep breath and began knocking on the door loudly.

After a minute of constant knocking, he heard a muffled voice demanding he stop. Abner stopped knocking and tightened his grip on the pistol. As soon as the door opened Abner was greeted by a drowsy irritated man. His face matched the profile of one of the terrorists. Before the man could speak, Abner aimed the silenced pistol at his face and shot him.

Abner quickly stepped over his body and entered the room, holding his pistol in front of him. He knew from doing reconnaissance that there were four of them in the apartment. He entered the living room silent as a ghost and saw one of them half asleep on the couch. Without a second thought he aimed his pistol at the sleeping man and shot him in the forehead. The guns suppressor had reduced the sound and flash of the gunshot to a barely audible squeak accompanied by a small puff of smoke.

"That's two," muttered Abner as he moved away from the living room. He could hear voices on the other side of the bedroom door whispering. He spun around and fired four shots at the bedroom door. The squeaks were instantaneously followed by the muffled thud of dead bodies hitting the floor. He walked into the room to make sure they were dead.

There were two of them, a man and a woman lying dead and bleeding on the floor. Abner smiled in grim satisfaction at a job well done as he returned his pistol to its holster. Abner returned to the living room. Sitting on a table was the terrorist's laptop he grabbed it and walked out of the room shutting the door behind him. Once he was back in the hallway, he removed his balaclava, and gloves. He walked to the elevator and rode it down to the lobby. Outside, it was still raining.

He ran across the street to the car, once inside, he put the laptop on the passenger seat next to him. Then he pulled out his pistol and returned the magazine, ammo and silencer to the tray. Finally, he pushed the tray back into place. Feeling relieved that it was over he pulled out his cellphone and dialed a number in Tel Aviv.

"Yes HOPLITE?" asked Director Yossi.

"Targets have been liquidated. Have obtained hostiles computer proceeding to airport now" said Abner.

"Excellent work, HOPLITE" said Director Yossi before hanging up. Abner returned the phone to his pocket and drove to the airport.

Chapter 3
They

The time was 9:00 pm and it was time for the leaders of the Neutral Executive for Total World Order Regardless of Consequences, commonly referred to as the Networc, to meet via teleconference. There were eight of them in total and they were known as the Board of Directors. Each member of the Board was assigned a codename of Mr. followed by a number from zero to seven. The head of the Board, and the Networcs commander in chief, was Mr. Zero. Each board member was a CEO of a different major multinational corporation serving as various branches of the Networc.

The Networc was divided into three branches: The Board of Directors which oversaw all aspects of the organization. The second branch was the Upper Echelon whose operatives represented the Networc and also carried out covert missions and collected intelligence on orders from board members. Members of the Upper Echelon are exclusively referred to as Counselor followed by a randomly chosen codename. The third branch was the Networcs military known as the Lower Echelon. The Lower Echelon consisted of mercenaries that were employees of the Networcs military branch known to the outside world as the private military company: Applied Dynamics.

Mr. Zero, the CEO of Kronos International which served as the Networcs manufacturing division, turned on his webcam which scrambled his and every board members voice and image so they could be unidentifiable. In order to ensure privacy none of the board members knew the identities of each other except for Mr. Zero. Next to his computer was a glass of Dom Perignon, he took a sip before glancing at his computer. On the screen were seven windows, each had the codename of a board member on it. "Welcome, gentlemen, let's get down to business" he said, his voice scrambled electronically.

"I think we should discuss the Kane problem first," said Mr. One, the CEO of Applied Dynamics.

Mr. Zero sighed, annoyed at this subject since it had been coming up more and more at Board meetings.

"I agree, it is because of him and his team that Project Big Picture was a failure" added Mr. Three, the CEO of Bloodstone Incorporated which served as the Networcs energy and construction branch.

"I concur, as long as he's alive he's dangerous," agreed Mr. Four, the CEO of the Networcs shipping division known as Windwaker Transports.

"He also killed Counselor Black, for that alone he must be eliminated" said Mr. Seven, the CEO of the Networcs global communications division known as Minute Broadcasting.

"Do we even know where he is?" asked Mr. Six, CEO of the Networcs Legal division aka the law firm of Wilburscheid and Hammelin.

"Yes, he's in Tangier with the daughter of the Triads leader," said Mr. Zero. "I've had the Upper Echelon keep an eye on him."

"Personally, I consider him to be a minor annoyance to us and besides we have more important things to focus on.... like Project: MOSES" said Mr. Zero. "And speaking of Project MOSES, what is the current status of the project, Mr. Five?"

Mr. Five was the CEO of King Midas Holdings which acted as the Networcs financial branch. "Everything is proceeding according to plan, at least on our end" he answered.

"What about the bomb?" asked Mr. Zero.

"We finished development of it last week. According to our technicians it should be powerful enough to destroy the Dam," answered Mr. Two.

Mr. Two served as the CEO of the Networcs Research and Development division known to the world as Prometheus Technologies.

"And the UEF, Mr. One?" asked Mr. Zero inquisitively.

Mr. One was silent for a few seconds as he thought about the answer. "Everything has gone fine, except for one tiny part," he responded.

"Several days ago, we intercepted a communiqué from someone in the Egyptian military regarding the UEF," answered Mr. One.

"Who was this "someone?" Mr. Two inquired.

"We don't know for sure, but we think it was Mossad," answered Mr. One.

"What do they know?" asked Mr. Five.

"Relax Mr. Five, they know nothing about us, all they know is the location of the bombing and we've taken precautions to ensure that the bombing cannot be traced back to us," countered Mr. One.

"It doesn't matter anyway the Israelis won't do anything, at least not directly," said Mr. Zero confidently.

"How do you know?" asked Mr. Two.

"They have more important matters to attend to, namely the riots we've been instigating behind the scenes in Gaza," said Mr. Zero. "As for Simon Kane, I will dispatch Counselor Cathcart to Tangier to take care of him."

Across the world the various members of the board nodded, placated at Mr. Zero's decision regarding Simon Kane. "Now then, I believe that's everything gentlemen, so I hereby call this meeting adjourned" said Mr. Zero.

Mr. Zero hung up and one by one the other board members hung up in response leaving a blank computer screen. Mr. Zero pulled his cellphone out of his pocket and dialed a certain number. After a few seconds of ringing there was an answer. "Counselor Cathcart this is Mr. Zero we have another target. His name is Simon Kane, at the moment he is in Tangier, your orders are to find and kill him."

"Understood," said Counselor Cathcart before hanging up.

Mr. Zero returned the phone to his pocket. He smiled at the impending success of Project: MOSES and the impending death of Simon Kane and took another sip of wine.

"It's good to be the king," muttered Mr. Zero as he looked out the window of his office.

Chapter 4
Stay the Hand

Hidden under the city of Tel Aviv in Israel, was a secret branch of the Institute for Intelligence and Special Operations, known to the world as Mossad. Known only to its members and the Israeli Prime Minister the branch was referred to as Golem. It specialized in covert missions and assassinations throughout the world, some called groups like it Shadow Agencies. Its agents were taken from the best of the Israeli Special Forces and as such were among the deadliest and most effective secret agents on Earth. The agency was led by an enigmatic woman known only as Director Yossi.

Abner Cohen, codename: HOPLITE, walked down the hall to Director Yossi's office eager to find out what they had found on the computer. He was a tall athletic man dressed in a blue blazer, black shirt with no tie and blue pants, his black hair was unkempt from a lack of sleep. He had been an agent of Golem for years after being recruited into Mossad from the IDF Special Forces. He knocked on the door of Director Yossi's office, she beckoned him to enter. Against the rear wall of her office was her desk. On the wall behind the desk was a frame with a tattered Israeli flag inside.

In front of the desk were two chairs, on the right side of the office was a series of bookcases and filing cabinets. On the left side was a massive computer screen that dominated the wall. Abner sat down in one of the chairs in front of the desk. Director Yossi sat behind the desk in her swivel chair looking at the flag on the wall behind her.

When Abner sat down in the seat, Director Yossi spun around to face him. She was an older woman of around fifty-six, her short red hair was combed to the left side. She was wearing a grey blazer with a dark blue dress shirt with the top three buttons undone revealing a gold necklace and a white dress with black heels. None of Abner's fellow agents knew much about her past though they had heard multiple, often conflicting stories. However, they were all positive that Yossi was not her real name.

"Welcome back, Cohen" said Director Yossi warmly.

"Thank you, ma'am, it's nice to be back," Abner replied.

"I know you're wondering what we found on that computer," said Director Yossi with a grin.

"Well, it has been on my mind," said Cohen sarcastically.

Director Yossi smirked at the sarcasm. "I'm sure, based on what we recovered from the computer your work is far from done," said Director Yossi.

"Is it ever done?" asked Abner sarcastically.

"Get serious Cohen," she snapped. "This is bigger than what you or any of us thought," continued Director Yossi.

"How so?" asked Abner. Director Yossi picked a small remote off her desk and aimed it at the large screen on the other side of the room. She pressed a button and a satellite image of Egypt appeared on screen.

"We're still analyzing that computer, however, a new problem popped up while you were shooting Nazis in Berlin, that requires our attention" answered Yossi.

Abner couldn't help but feel intrigued. For as long as Abner had been a member of Golem tracking down and killing Aquarius members had been a priority. "Must be pretty big, to take priority over Aquarius," he observed.

"It is. Forty-eight hours ago, our man in Cairo told us that an Egyptian Special Forces unit had gone rogue and formed a terrorist group calling themselves the United Egyptian Front or UEF for short," explained Yossi.

"Catchy name," said Abner sardonically.

"They're led by a man named General Omar Faisel. He's a hard-line radical who wants to finish what Sadat and the Arabs started in 73." continued Director Yossi, ignoring his humor.

"Naturally the Egyptians are keeping this quiet," continued Director Yossi. "To make matters worse, we believe the UEF have acquired a GBU-43 bomb from Egypt's stockpile with the intention of using it to destroy the Aswan Dam."

"The UEF will then blame it on us triggering a war between our countries," continued Director Yossi.

"Have to admit, I didn't see that coming," grunted Abner.

"We have been keeping an eye on Faisel for some time due to his history. We believe the attack will happen next week, possibly on Friday," said Yossi.

"I assume you want me to go down there and stop them?" asked Abner expecting a yes.

"No, the Prime minister and the President both vetoed that idea" replied Director Yossi.

"Why?!" asked Abner perplexed at the answer.

"We're in the middle of some delicate negotiations with the Egyptians which obviously nixes sending in any of our agents right now," explained Director Yossi.

Abner was about to speak when Director Yossi held up her hand. "Wait" barked Director Yossi. "I said none of "our" agents."

"What are you getting at?" Abner asked.

"The President and Prime Minister both agree that we cannot allow the UEF to carry out an attack like this" said Director Yossi. "However, we can't send you or anyone else in and we can't notify the Egyptians without potentially warning the UEF."

"However, there is a third option that will keep both our hands clean" continued Director Yossi.

"Which is?" asked Abner.

"Do you remember a Silhouette agent named Simon Kane?" asked Director Yossi.

Abner shook his head. "Several years ago, you worked with him and two other Silhouette agents in Beirut" said Director Yossi.

"Sounds familiar" answered Abner.

"Maybe this will help," said Director Yossi as she pressed a button on the remote and a picture of Simon Kane's head flashed on screen. His black hair was gelled back, a clean shaven, rough yet handsome face and a slight tan. His left eye was a dark green, his right eye was covered by a black eye patch.

Abner studied the picture for a minute. "Now I do, married a fellow agent, right?"

"Yes, now for reasons unknown, he's no longer a member of Silhouette and has instead been running across the world with this Chinese philanthropist" said Director Yossi.

"At the moment they're in Tangier doing God knows what" said Director Yossi.

"And you intend to get him to stop the attack?" asked Abner.

"Exactly" replied Director Yossi with a snap of her fingers.

"Why not use Mosaic?" asked Abner skeptical of the plan.

"Number One, Simon Kane is closer and number two Mosaic has close ties to Silhouette and I don't want them finding out about this" answered Director Yossi.

"How do you know he won't tell Silhouette?" asked Abner.

"Because they're probably looking for him with intentions to kill him ever since he left," answered Director Yossi.

"And how do you intend to get him from Tangier to Aswan?" asked Abner.

"Have you ever heard of Cobalt Incorporated?" replied Director Yossi.

"Yeah, they're arms dealers, right?" answered Abner.

"Indeed," said Director Yossi as she pressed a button on the remote and Simon's picture vanished from the screen. The picture was replaced with an image of two women, a man and the logo for a company named Cobalt Incorporated. One of the women had dark brown skin, spiky black hair and the muscular body of a soldier. She was dressed in blue jeans and a black sleeveless shirt. The man was bald with a strong physique and white skin. He was dressed in a long sleeve black shirt and light brown khakis.

Standing in between them was a younger, very attractive woman in a suit. She had long black hair with a narrow white streak running down the left side. Her skin was devoid of pigmentation making it chalk white and giving her an almost ghostly ethereal appearance.

"The woman in the middle is Gretchen Neubauer, an arms dealer like her father," said Director Yossi.

"Is there a reason why she looks like Caspar the friendly ghost's hot sister?" asked Abner sarcastically.

Director Yossi grinned at his wording knowing exactly what he was referencing. "She was born with a rare form of albinism resulting in a lack of skin pigmentation as well as that white streak in her hair."

"And the other two?" asked Abner. "Her bodyguards, the black woman is Naomi Grant and the white guy is her husband, Scott" answered Director Yossi. "According to our files both of them are ex-British Royal Marines that were recruited by Neubauer a few years ago when she was setting up Cobalt Incorporated," she continued.

"We've recruited them to transport Kane to Aswan," said Director Yossi.

"So where do I come in?" Abner asked.

"You will fly out to Cobalt's HQ in Greece with a file containing our intel on Simon Kane and the mission" answered Director Yossi.

"That's it?" asked Abner.

"Not even close, once that's done you are to fly to Aswan and await their arrival and brief him on the situation as well as provide him with anything he needs to stop them," replied Director Yossi.

"It seems too risky," responded Abner.

"In our line of work everything is risky, and to be frank I don't like it either but the President and Prime Minister like it," answered Director Yossi.

"So, it's the best bad idea we've got then?" said Abner.

"Do you have any other ideas? Besides we don't have time to come up with a better one" the Director replied bluntly.

"What about the risk of us being exposed?" inquired Abner.

"The risk is minimal; Cobalt thinks we're a defense company called Tri-Mark securities" answered Director Yossi.

Abner wasn't surprised to hear the name Tri-Mark securities since it was essentially a Golem front specializing in intelligence collection and private security.

"I can tell you don't like the plan," said Director Yossi.

Abner was surprised since he didn't think his disapproval was that obvious. "To be honest ma'am, I don't like it, there are too many variables and a lack of control on our part."

"Is that so? Well here's the thing, Cohen you're not paid to like it," grunted Director Yossi.

Abner sighed, realizing his protests had fallen on uncaring ears. "When do I leave?" asked Abner.

"That's the spirit, your booked on the 2:30 flight to Athens," answered Director Yossi. She picked up two file folders off her desk and handed them to him. "Here ares the files on Kane you're to give Neubauer" she said as Abner took the folders.

"They've been edited to remove any mention of us or Silhouette" said Director Yossi.

"Makes sense, it would be bad politics to spill the CIA's secrets" said Abner as he flipped through the folder. "Smart man, anyway your dismissed, HOPLITE" said Director Yossi.

"Yes ma'am," said Abner as he stood up.

As soon as he was out of her office and the door had shut behind him, he punched the wall out of rage. This is bullshit, I should be doing this not some mercenary he thought. He shifted his attention to the pain in his hand.

"So be it" muttered Abner.

"If he fails, I'll find him and shoot him myself" muttered Abner.

Chapter 5
Moonlight over Spy City

Simon Kane stood on the balcony of their hotel room admiring the view. The sun was setting, turning the clouds above into wisps of orange and red. Below, the city of Tangier was a glittering mass of lights that seemed to go on forever. Three and a half hours away was Casablanca, where Simon and Sheila fell in love on a mission. Simon closed his eye and smiled at the memory. They would go to a little restaurant every morning and spend the day at the beach then enjoy the nightlife.

He'd been to Casablanca a few times in the years since, but it wasn't the same without her. The cool night air of the desert wafted into their room refreshingly. Simon walked away from the balcony and back into the living room. It was one of the more expensive and luxurious rooms in the hotel.

He was wearing his black shirt and dark green pants; his wrist blade was on the coffee table. Mai was in the bedroom resting after spending almost all day working at refugee shelters. Simon wasn't as tired, but he was still glad she was done working. He sat down on the couch which had doubled as his bed while they were staying in the room. Lacking anything better to do, he removed his pistol, a Jericho 941, from his shoulder holster and he started checking it.

Suddenly the bedroom door opened, and Mai walked out into the living room. Instinctively Simon placed his gun on the coffee table in front of him and turned around. Having just woken up she was still wearing her sleeping clothes, a white tank top and light pink underwear. As she walked over to Simon, she was rubbing her eyes drowsily. "How'd you sleep?" he asked.

"Fine, mostly," replied Mai groggily.

"It was the dream again, wasn't it?" Simon asked.

Mai sat next to Simon on the couch, leaned forward and buried her face in her hands. Simon could tell what the answer was already. She took a deep breath, "they're getting worse and worse," she said.

Simon placed his hand on Mai's shoulder comfortingly. He knew what Mai was suffering from, he had seen many suffer through it during his time in SEAL team Six and as a Silhouette agent. They both knew the dreams were a direct result of Mai being almost being raped during their escape from Sankan two and a half months ago.

"Is there anything I can do to help?" asked Simon gently.

Mai stubbornly shook her head. "I just keep reliving that night over and over again. In the dream I see those two men, the little one grabbing me and the big one beating you to death," said Mai starting to cry.

"I feel like such a coward," she moaned, her head buried in her hands.

Simon hated seeing her like this, even though he had rescued her from the cartel's clutches on Sankan. Even though both of those men were killed before they could satisfy their demented urges, she still was haunted by the trauma of that night.

"Bull," said Simon bluntly.

She looked up at him confused her face damp with tears. "What?" asked Mai weakly.

"You're no coward, hell you're one of the bravest people I've ever met," said Simon.

"How?" asked Mai skeptically.

"A coward would not do any of the things I've seen you do," said Simon. "A coward would not go to the dangerous hellholes we've been to without a second thought for their own safety."

"A coward wouldn't drive like a bat out of hell through the streets of Sankan while being chased by trigger happy bikers," said Simon in an effort to comfort her.

"My driving isn't that bad," said Mai with a faint smile as she wiped the tears from her eyes.

"You sure about that?" said Simon as he cracked a smile.

Mai smiled at the wisecrack her tears replaced with a mild laugh.

"If there's one thing I've learned over the years it's that real bravery isn't the absence of fear, but the ability to overcome fear" continued Simon.

Mai leaned in close to him and wrapped her arms around him. Simon was caught off guard by the hug, but he held her for support anyway.

"Thanks Simon, I needed that" said Mai, her head resting on his shoulder.

"Anytime" said Simon.

Slowly they released each other from the mutual embrace. As Mai leaned away from him, her arms falling to the couch, their eyes locked onto each other. During their time together Mai had slowly developed feelings for Simon. Feelings she was unsure of and tried to keep hidden by reminding herself that he was just a bodyguard recruited by her gangster father, interested only in revenge.

Mai would often remind herself that they were nothing alike. She was a pacifist, an educated humanitarian and he was a soldier, a killer of men. But then she would realize that there were as many similarities between them as there were differences. When they first met, she just assumed he was another brain dead American but she was wrong. He was an educated man who had dedicated his life to delivering punishment to those who would hurt the innocent.

She also detected a certain vulnerability to him that he tried to mask with humor. Though she had to admit, despite the eye patch, he was an attractive man as she looked at him now in the cool light of the room. She was surprised at how much muscle he had, after brushing up against his muscles during their momentary embrace. His smoothed back black hair and black eye patch combined together to give him a rugged yet oddly sophisticated appearance. Simon was surprised at how gorgeous Mai looked without her glasses on.

Gone were the trappings of a geeky secretary. Now she looked almost like a model in her white tank top and light pink underwear which accentuated her curvaceous body. Her smooth skin glistened in the moonlight that filtered into the room. Neither of them knew what to call it but they could both feel it, the electricity between them fanned by flames deep within them both. Slowly they moved closer to each other until noses were touching. Their hearts were beating in unison, furiously with disbelief and emotion as their lips drew closer and closer to each other.

"Anytime?" asked Mai seductively.

"Anytime" replied Simon quietly.

They could control themselves no longer.

They closed their eyes as their lips met each other. They wrapped their arms around each other in a loving embrace. Mai's hand glided through his jet-black hair as they held each other tightly consumed by passion.

Simon's hands were on her back occasionally drifting up to the back of her neck. Slowly he began to lean against the armrest with Mai on top of him as they continued to kiss and caress each other's bodies passionately.

Suddenly Mai's eyes opened, and she leaned up away from him and sat away from him. Simon, feeling somewhat confused, sat up and looked at her. He tried to think of something to say but couldn't. As if she could sense his confusion, Mai looked at him and her eyes started to water.

"I'm sorry, it's just...I don't," stammered Mai, she took a deep breath and closed her eyes.

"I just can't, considering what's happened and I need to sort this out okay? Just give me some time" said Mai.

Simon placed his hand on her shoulder comfortingly. "It's okay...really, hell I'm not in the mood anyway" said Simon with a smirk.

She grinned. "Liar" said Mai, she stood up and walked back to her room.

Before she closed the door, she snuck a look at Simon before closing the door behind her. Simon leaned back in the couch and whistled feeling emotionally drained. He walked over to the balcony to think, he leaned forward on the railing resting his arms on it. The sky was black with a smattering of stars while the city below was a glittering cornucopia of life and sound. He asked himself why Mai couldn't continue and came to two conclusions.

He had a feeling that what they were doing like that reminded her too much of that night in Sankan. The other conclusion was that she was starting to fall in love with him and he with her. He shuddered at the possibility, after Sheila died, he swore to himself that he would never fall in love with anyone again. While he did have feelings for Mai, he knew that if he acted on them she might end up like Sheila one day. He knelt his head on the railing of the balcony. After tonight there was no ignoring his feelings for her. He squeezed his fist more out of frustration than anger.

"Dammit," muttered Simon.

Chapter 6
The Athenian Connection

Abner Cohen didn't know whether it was Yossi or Cobalt that decided on meeting at the Parthenon, but he was glad they did regardless.

One of his hobbies was studying ancient mythology, antiquity and civilizations. His favorite civilization to study had to be ancient Greece. He had read multiple books on it and attended lectures at Haifa University. He often asked himself why he didn't become a history professor instead of a spy. The only answer he could think of was the adventure inherent to the job.

Still the best part of the job had to be the travel and nowhere was that more true than this morning in Athens. He had already memorized everything in the dossier Director Yossi gave him. According to the dossier, he was supposed to meet a representative of Cobalt Incorporated at the front of the Parthenon at ten in the morning. He intentionally showed up an hour early so he could walk around the Parthenon. It was a beautiful morning to be outside, the sky was a bright blue and the warm rays of sunlight were bouncing off the ruins.

Abner was dressed in dark blue pants, a black dress shirt and a dark blue blazer. He carried a black briefcase containing the documents he was to give to Neubauer. He regretted that he couldn't bring his gun with him, however, he felt confident that he could defend himself if he had to. He had been walking around the temple on the northern side of the structure when he decided to check his watch. He grunted in annoyance at the time, nine fifty-five AM. He walked away from the temple to the entrance of the Parthenon for the rendezvous.

He leaned against one of the ancient stone pillars and waited for the contact to arrive. He would know his contact when he or she uttered a certain code word and vice versa. Director Yossi told him that he would be meeting one of the three Cobalt members but not which member specifically. He assumed it would be one of the two bodyguards. He scanned the crowds of people for one of them but didn't see them.

Suddenly a hand placed itself on his shoulder. "Got a light," said a man with a thick British accent behind him. Instinctively, Abner turned around to face him, he recognized the man as Scott Grant.

Having heard the proper codeword Abner delivered the proper remark confirming his identity. "Sorry, I don't smoke, bad for my health" replied Abner dismissively, the man grinned.

"What isn't," replied the man as he tossed the unlit cigarette to the ground.

With that response the man had confirmed his identity. Abner felt relieved that this was not an ambush. "You must be the contact from Israel, names Scott" said the man as he extended his hand politely.

"Yes, call me HOPLITE," replied Abner as the two men shook hands. He studied the man's appearance having seen him up close. Scott was a large muscular bald Caucasian man wearing a gray member's only jacket with a t shirt under it with the logo of the Chelsea football club on it and blue jeans.

"Is that the stuff?" asked Grant gesturing to the briefcase.

Abner nodded in the affirmative. "Smashing, shall we go?" asked Grant.

"Lead the way, so why didn't Neubauer come, she paranoid?" he asked as he followed Scott to the parking lot.

"Naw mate, she's sleeping back at the mansion" replied Grant as they arrived at his car, a black SUV. Before Abner could respond Grant turned around to face him. "I'm gonna have to give you a pat down before we go any further mate."

Abner held out his arms and Grant searched him. "Satisfied?"

"Yeah, let's go," said Grant nonchalantly and stood up. He opened the front passenger door of the SUV and motioned for Abner to get inside. Abner got in the car and placed the briefcase on his lap. Grant got in the driver's seat and drove away, the Parthenon growing smaller the farther they went.

*****

Naomi Grant often marveled at the bizarre path her life had taken as she walked up the stairs of the mansion to wake up Gretchen. From the Royal Marines to working as bodyguard for a woman who trafficked in tools of death and destruction. She sighed, mildly annoyed as she walked up the stairs of the mansion. It wasn't the first time she had to wake Gretchen up and she knew it wouldn't be the last. Naomi was already dressed in a black suit and tie for the meeting.

She arrived at the door to Gretchen's bedroom and knocked on it loudly, feeling like a mother waking up children for school. "Gretchen! It's time to get up. Scott's on his way here with the client" she barked.

After hearing no response, she opened the door and walked in. "Bloody hell you're not even dressed yet" said Naomi in her stern

English accent upon seeing Gretchen lying on her bed half-asleep.

Gretchen was wearing a white t shirt and red underwear. She grunted in annoyance at the abrupt wake up call. "I know, I know" she said lethargically in her thick German accent which only accentuated her quirkiness.

Reluctantly she rolled out of bed and rubbed her eyes. "I'd hurry if I were you" said Naomi as she walked to the closet and removed Gretchen's suit.

"What would I do without you Naomi?" muttered Gretchen as she looked in the mirror.

"Best not to think about that," replied Naomi as she casually laid her clothes on the bed.

While Gretchen got dressed, Naomi caught a glimpse of the blue dragon tattoo that ran down the left side of her back, its origin unknown even to Naomi and her husband.

Naomi looked around Gretchen's room, maybe it was because of her time in the military but she was utterly repulsed by Gretchen's bedroom. It was a disorganized mass of entertainment magazines, file folders and clothes.

"I'm ready" said Gretchen as she finished dressing herself.

She was wearing a white blazer with a red tie and black dress shirt and a white skirt with black heels. Her porcelain skin was so white it was hard to tell where her white sleeves ended, and her skin began.

Naomi looked up at her studying her appearance. She shrugged in disapproval. "No, you're not" corrected Naomi. "Your hair is unkempt."

Gretchen sighed annoyed at her omission and subsequent chastisement. She turned to face the mirror and quickly brushed her hair so that she looked more professional. "Better?" she asked.

"Much better," replied Naomi.

"Ausgezeichnet," said Gretchen with a smile. "When are they going to arrive?"

As if in answer the front doorbell rang. "I'd say now," said Naomi slyly.

"Great timing" said Gretchen sarcastically. "Let's go" she said as they walked out of her room to the front door.

They arrived at the front door and opened it, standing in the doorway were Scott and Abner. "Welcome to Greece!" said Gretchen excitedly holding out her arms in a welcoming manner.

"Ms. Neubauer," said Abner, surprised by her enthusiasm.

It was hard for him to believe that the attractive young woman with the pale skin and hourglass figure was one of the world's biggest arms dealers. He remembered reading in her file that she had a reputation for being unpredictable and childish as well as being a brilliant strategist and negotiator. "By the way what am I supposed to call you, the company didn't give me your name?" asked Gretchen.

"HOPLITE" answered Abner dryly.

"Like the ancient Greek soldiers?" asked Gretchen.

Abner nodded in the affirmative. "Sehr Cool," said Gretchen with her cheshire grin.

"You've already met Scott so allow me to introduce you to my other guard Mrs. Naomi Grant" continued Gretchen gesturing to Naomi.

Abner and Naomi shook hands, Abner studied Naomi carefully, she was a tall attractive black woman with short black hair and the muscular frame and posture of a soldier. He noticed that both Scott and Naomi had wedding rings on their right fingers, which was unusual given their profession.

"Now that we've made the introductions let us retire to the patio and discuss business," said Gretchen.

"Fine with me," said Abner as he followed Gretchen across the mansion. Behind them were Scott and Naomi.

"Scott, Naomi wait here," said Gretchen upon arriving at the patio door.

They nodded and walked off as Gretchen opened the door. Abner followed her through the door to a table sitting on the patio next to the pool. Abner placed his briefcase on the table before sitting down across the table from Gretchen.

"I must say I never expected to get a job from Tri-Mark Securities," said Gretchen.

"And I never expected to rely on a twenty-two-year-old German arms dealer and her pet Royal Marines," replied Abner.

"Just how much do you know about us?" asked Gretchen leaning back in her chair.

"Plenty, for example you were born in Hanover, Germany," answered Abner.

"Your father was the international arms dealer, Arnold Neubauer. After his death you used his resources and contacts to set up Cobalt Incorporated five years ago," continued Abner. "Since then you and your bodyguards have been spotted across the world selling weapons to anyone with money."

"As for your bodyguards, Naomi Grant was born in London to Jamaican parents". "She joined the Royal Marines at seventeen where she met and later married Scott Grant," continued Abner. "As for him, he was born in Shirebrook Derbyshire in England where he had a nasty habit of getting into barfights as a teenager."

"At sixteen he joined the Royal Marines where he met Naomi," continued Abner. "After they got married, they left the Marines and were flat broke" said Abner.

"That is until you recruited them to be your bodyguards four years ago, now did I miss anything?" finished Abner with a sarcastic smile.

Gretchen sighed, looking rather entertained at having her life read back to her. "So, you know about us then, well what about you?" she asked.

"Not important, what is important is this," said Abner as he opened the briefcase, removed a folder, marked Kane, and handed it to Gretchen.

"That folder contains all the intel we have on the terrorist attack, Simon Kane and his companion," said Abner. Gretchen opened the folder and began skimming through it, carefully reading its contents.

"This Simon Kane, he's kinda hot, even with the eye patch," said Gretchen as she looked up at Abner.

"Everybody has a preference. Do you need anything else?" asked Abner.

"A few answers to a few questions. Like is the gun truck on site?" asked Gretchen, as she placed the folder on the table. She slouched forward and rested her head on her right hand lazily.

"By the time you get there yes along with the equipment. We sent them to the address you gave us in Tangier" answered Abner.

"Good, now I've noticed that the details of the attack, among other things, have been crossed out of the folder, why?" asked Gretchen.

"Need to know," replied Abner.

"I see, now what about our payment?" asked Gretchen. "I noticed that there's no cash in that briefcase" she observed as her eyes darted to the briefcase and back to Abner.

"You will be paid upon arriving in Aswan with Simon" he answered.

Gretchen frowned at the answer. She stood up and walked over to him and sat down on the table in front of him, her legs swinging back and forth. "Have you ever seen Scarface Mr. HOPLITE?"

"Yes. Your point?" answered Abner.

She placed her hands on the edge of the table and stared directly at him as if right into his soul with her piercing red eyes. "You see there's a line from that movie that I think is applicable to this situation of ours"

"What's the line?" asked Abner.

Gretchen leaned in close to him her face as serious as murder. "Don't fuck me, Don't you ever try to fuck me"

They looked at each other sternly for almost a full minute, sizing each other up. Suddenly Gretchen leaned away from him and held her arms up smiling. "I mean I know I look good, but you're just not my type" said Gretchen.

Abner cracked a smile as he stood up knowing that she was really sending a message. "That cuts both ways."

"Then we don't have a problem," said Gretchen as she slid off the table and shook hands.

Abner picked up his briefcase and followed her back inside to the front door.

"There's a taxi outside waiting for you" said Gretchen as she opened the front door.

"Good luck" said Abner before walking out the door.

Gretchen closed the door and locked it, "he's gone."

In response Naomi and Scott walked into the living room.

"What did you find?" asked Gretchen anxiously.

"While you were talking, I did some checking and he's on the level, worked for Tri-Mark Securities for seven years," said Naomi.

"And Tri Mark?" asked Gretchen. "Again, they're legit, the only thing in question is the motive," said Naomi.

"I don't like it. This job is getting way too wiggy way too fast," said Gretchen nervously. "Then again I like it when shit gets wiggy, it's more fun," said Gretchen gleefully.

She put one arm on Naomi's shoulder and one arm on Scotts shoulder.

"Pack your bags kids, we're going to Tangier!" said Gretchen.

She removed her arms from them and walked up to her room.

Naomi and Scott looked at each other, "I guess we're going to Tangier" said Scott dryly.

"I don't like how that guy knew all about us" said Naomi nervously.

"I know luv, neither do I" replied Scott.

"Anyway, let's get packed up. I'll go make the arrangements" said Scott as he walked away to the office.

Naomi walked outside to the patio and picked up the folder and studied the picture of Simon Kane.

"I don't like this," muttered Naomi.

Chapter 7
Means To An End

The Café Panorama restaurant was located across the street from the beach. The ocean glistened in the late morning sunlight. It was not hard to understand why the beaches of Tangier had a reputation for being among the most beautiful in the Mediterranean. The palm trees wafted gently in the wind while people swam and tanned. The streets were filled with the bustling masses common to beachside cities.

Simon and Mai sat in the outside dining area of the café quietly eating breakfast. Simon was reading a magazine while Mai was on her phone. Mai took a deep breath and looked up from her phone.

"So...about last night," said Mai nervously.

In response Simon looked up from his magazine. He had been hoping she wouldn't bring up the events of last night.

"I feel like we should talk about it," she continued as she straightened her glasses. "Look, you once told me that the only thing you gave a damn about is avenging your wife."

"And I remember that I also said once I had gotten it, I would disappear" replied Simon as he tossed the magazine on the table.

She nodded, "Well, I have to know if that is still true, am I just some job for you?" asked Mai.

"I could ask you the same thing" said Simon calmly. He saw her raise an eyebrow in both surprise and confusion. "Think about it, I'm here to protect you in case one of your father's enemies tries something while you're doing your charity work. So by that logic aren't I just a means to your end?"

Mai sat quietly methodically examining what he had said. "You're not just a means to an end."

"Well if I'm not a means to an end then what am I to you?" he asked. Somewhere deep down, Simon wanted her to say she loved him, but he knew she couldn't say it and neither could he.

Mai was quiet for a minute as she looked down into her coffee cup thinking. She looked up at him from her coffee, a stern serious look on her face. "Say what you want Simon, but last night on the couch you could feel it and so could I."

He shrugged. "Let me ask you something Mai" said Simon. "How do you think this is going to end? After I've gotten my revenge, you and I go live happily ever after?"

"Well I've been there, I've done that and I got the lousy damn t shirt" said Simon.

"Now I get it, this is really about her then," replied Mai. "I don't know the whole story but I understand now," she said with a confident grin.

"You're afraid to get close to anyone because of what happened to her," said Mai smugly.

Simon sighed knowing that deep down in his soul she was right. "I didn't know you were a shrink" said Simon sarcastically.

"I don't have to be one to see it. Frankly I feel stupid for not realizing it sooner" Mai replied, ignoring his flippant remark. "But the funny thing is that you do love me or at the very least you care more about me than you're letting on."

Simon grinned dryly and laughed softly. Sheila used to pull this same routine with him. "So, am I gonna get a bill for this psychoanalysis session of yours?"

"Make all the jokes you want, you know I'm right about last night and about you," answered Mai.

"Either way, it doesn't matter" said Simon dismissively.

Mai raised her hands in frustration and laughed. "You can't admit it, I swear you are the most stubborn man I have ever met."

"That's quite a compliment coming from you," replied Simon with a sly grin.

"Let's go" said Mai with an annoyed grunt. "

You're the boss" he replied.

The two of them stood up and walked to the counter, paid for their food then walked to their car. The car was on the second floor of a parking garage down the street. It was a giant grey edifice with five floors. They walked to the parking garage quietly with Simon keeping close to Mai and scanning the crowds for potential assassins. As they walked Mai tried to think of something to say.

Upon entering the garage Mai turned to face him. "Simon…I," she began.

"Not now," barked Simon before she could finish.

"What is it?" asked Mai nervously. She could tell from the deadly serious look on Simons face and the sudden gruffness in his voice the severity of the situation.

"Someone's following us, probably since we left the café," said Simon as he pulled out his Jericho and cocked it.

Mai looked around and listened more carefully than she ever had but she heard or saw nothing. "Where are they? I don't see anything" she asked.

"Trust me they're here. I guess around two maybe three" said Simon as he quickly scanned their surroundings.

Mai sometimes forgot that Simon was a former CIA agent and Navy SEAL making his senses much sharper than hers. Slowly they began to inch toward the staircase and that led to the second floor of the garage and their salvation. Suddenly Simon saw movement near one of the cars out of the corner of his eye. He swung around and fired two bullets at the shape followed by an audible groan and the thud of a body hitting the floor and someone running. *Got one of them at least,* reasoned Simon.

"Mai! Run upstairs to the car! Now! Don't stop!" he yelled.

"What about you?" asked Mai.

"Did I stutter? Move!" barked Simon his eye locked on Mai as he slowly backed up.

Mai nodded and ran as fast as she could. Simon could hear footsteps approaching from the other side of the garage. He swung around and fired two more shots at the person, then ran up the stairs. Upon arriving at the top of the stairs he stopped, transfixed at the sight before him. Standing in front of him was a large bald white man dressed in brown khaki pants and a black t-shirt. Lying motionless in his burly arms was Mai, her body limp and lifeless.

"Easy way or the hard way mate. Your choice?" said the man in a thick British accent.

"How about my way," said Simon as he instinctively raised the pistol at the man's head. *Bastard is too big to dodge the bullet and there's nothing for him to jump behind so the only thing I need to worry about is his partner,* thought Simon.

Suddenly, he felt a sharp sting on the back of his neck. Instinctively Simon lowered his pistol and placed a hand on the source of the sting and felt a dart. He spun around as his legs began to give way and saw a black woman, with short hair dressed in a black tank top and blue jeans. She walked towards him holding a small pistol in her hand. Within seconds Simon was on the ground.

"Shit" muttered Simon before he lost consciousness.

"Nice shot Luv, what should we do with her?" asked Scott gesturing to Mai.

"Put her in the van with him. No need to kill her if we don't have to" said Naomi. She pulled her phone out of her pocket and dialed a number while Scott slung Simon. After a few seconds of ringing she got an answer.

"Yes?" said Gretchen over the phone.

"Objectives Yin and Yang have been recovered, heading to rally point lima," said Naomi.

"And the local muscle," Gretchen asked.

"KIA" said Naomi bluntly.

"Too bad. Proceed" she replied before hanging up.

Naomi returned the phone to her pocket and looked over at Scott. "Well?" he asked.

"Let's go, cops are on the way," Naomi ordered. The two walked over to their van and put the unconscious bodies of Mai and Simon in the back and drove off.

Watching them from behind one of the cars was a man cloaked in the shadows of the parking garage. He was dressed in a black dress shirt with a tie and pants with a silver belt, a black trench coat and a black fedora with a gray band and black gloves. As they left the garage, the man pulled out his cellphone and dialed the number of his superior. After the ringing, he heard the scrambled voice of his leader ask for an update.

"Mr. Zero, this is Counselor Cathcart, unknown forces have abducted Kane and Yunao, please advise" said the man in black.

"Observe and report. We can't afford to show our hand too soon" said Mr. Zero.

"Yes sir," replied Counselor Cathcart. Mr. Zero ended the call and returned the phone to his pocket and got in his car.

Chapter 8
A Take It Or Leave It Type Deal

Simon Kane awoke in a wooden chair his arms tied behind him with chains. His trench coat, his gun and wrist blade, were gone. He was glad to see he still had his watch. "Great. just what I needed another kidnapping."

Suddenly the door opened and into the room walked a white man and a black woman. Simon immediately recognized them as the two that had kidnapped him and Mai at the parking garage. "Allow us to introduce ourselves I'm Naomi" said the woman. "He's Scott" she continued, gesturing to the man.

"Good to know. Those names will definitely fit on your tombstones," growled Simon.

"You sure about that yank?" asked Scott, "because those chains imply otherwise."

"Four things are going to happen in the next five minutes," growled Simon. "First, I'm going to get out of these chains, second, I'm going to break his nose, third, I'm going to make you tell me where Mai is and depending on the answer I may or may not kill you"

"Fourth, her and I are going to get the hell out of here" continued Simon.

Scott and Naomi were silent for a few minutes; the silence was interrupted by the sound of hands clapping slowly.

"Ohhh, we got ourselves a badass over here," said a feminine voice in a heavy yet quirky German accent from outside the room.

An attractive young woman dressed in a white skirt, black dress shirt and a red striped tie walked into the room clapping her hands slowly. Her skin was as white as fresh snow, she had long black hair with a narrow white streak on the left side of it. She was easily shorter and younger than the man and the other two observed Simon. Scott and Naomi's eyes were locked on her as she walked into the room, a devilish smile on her face as her eyes were locked on Simon.

"Gretchen, you shouldn't be in here" said Scott sternly.

"Nahh, he's fine, besides I had to see this badass for myself," replied Gretchen dismissively. "And the minute I heard that four things speech I just had to see this cycloptic fuck for myself."

"Seriously, you don't get lines that good in Tarantino movies," laughed Gretchen. "I mean it, the attitude, the balls to the wall badassery and that goddamn eye patch, he's like Snake Plissken without the mullet,"

As she spoke Simon opened a secret compartment in his watch and removed a mini lock-pick. He maneuvered the pick into the lock on the chains taking care to not let them know what he was doing.

"Like, how do you not have your own action figure and Saturday morning cartoon?" said Gretchen. "And the icing on top is that he's hot, seriously this guy is freaking adorable!"

Simon had been called a lot of things over the years but adorable was not one of them. His thoughts raced as he tried to figure out who this woman was as he continued picking the lock. She had a strong German accent which ruled out Red Curtain, Silhouette and Equinox leaving only one possibility he reasoned. But as important as that was, he still had to ask the most important question. Either way he was getting tired of being ignored just as he managed to free himself.

He quickly jumped to his feet, wrapping the chain around his right hand and grabbed Gretchen, wrapping his left arm around her neck. He held her in front of him using her as a human shield. "Told you" he quipped.

"Oh...My...GOD!" Gretchen yelled. "It's like Christmas! Now he's taking me hostage and I can feel his muscles! Best day ever!" she said with an excited almost maniacal grin.

Instinctively, Scott and Naomi moved to free her from him, but he cracked the chain on the floor like a whip causing them to step back. "Tell dumbass and dipshit over there to step aside and take me to Mai" sneered Simon.

"I love this guy. However, I don't love being a hostage so Naomi if you will," said Gretchen.

Naomi sighed, pulled out a small dart gun and aimed it at Simon's left arm. She fired it at him and once again Simon felt his muscles loosen and before he knew it he fell on his back on the floor. "That dart contained a harmless paralytic, but you will still be able to talk."

"Good to know" growled Simon.

"Bitchin one liners too, seriously can I like put you in a jar and save you for a rainy day or something?" said Gretchen. "Oh shit, sorry I'm ranting I do that. Hi, my names Gretchen Neubauer, CEO and founder of Cobalt Incorporated," she said as she held out her hand and smiled.

"You'll forgive me if I don't shake hands," Simon grunted.

"And it gets even better he makes jokes!" yelled Gretchen as she excitedly threw her up her hands.

"Where's Mai?" growled Simon.

"Please," said Gretchen softly.

"What?" Simon asked utterly blindsided by both her response and how calmly she delivered it.

"Where's Mai please?" Gretchen clarified.

"Are you fucking serious?" asked Simon.

"Now, now is that any way to talk to a lady" said Gretchen.

"Psychos yes, ladies no. Ladies don't go sending their goons to kidnap people" replied Simon.

"And now he insults me! Seriously the file didn't mention anything about this guy being so damn adorable!" said Gretchen excitedly.

"I have officially lost patience with you people, where is Mai?" demanded Simon angrily.

"Just say the magic word" said Gretchen teasingly.

He sighed. "Please tell me where Mai is" asked Simon through gritted teeth.

"Now was that so hard?" Gretchen asked innocently.

Simon glared at her in response.

"Anyway, rest assured your Chinese girlfriend is fine she's just sedated in the other room," Gretchen explained.

"She's not my girlfriend" said Simon.

Gretchen smiled at the answer, "So you're single then? This day just went from a chocolate milkshake to a root beer float!" said Gretchen with a deranged smile gesticulating with her hands. "Shit now I'm hungry" she muttered lowering her hands, her tone returning to normal.

"Cobalt Incorporated, I've heard of you people. You're arms dealers" replied Simon.

"You say that like it's a bad thing" said Gretchen dismissively.

"Considering I've been kidnapped, chained up and paralyzed by you people I wonder why" said Simon.

Gretchen smiled impressed. "Touché, Mr. Kane."

"What's with the two Brits by the way?" he asked.

"They work for me. My bodyguards" explained Gretchen.

"For your sake they better be good" said Simon.

"Good enough to kidnap your yank ass" said Scott.

"Everyone gets lucky once" retorted Simon dismissively. "So, what do you want with me?" he asked shifting his attention to Gretchen.

"Your help. I'd be happy to tell you the details say...over dinner?" said Gretchen coquettishly.

"And if I'm not hungry?" Simon asked.

"Then you and Mai find out how tasty a bullet sandwich is" said Gretchen quietly.

Gretchen leaned in closely. "Hint not very."

Simon sighed more out of annoyance than defeat, though he felt relieved to know that Mai was still alive. He decided to play along for now. "What time?" asked Simon.

"Wunderbar, tonight at eight, Scott and Naomi will show you and Mai to your rooms" said Gretchen.

She looked at Scott and Naomi and gestured to Simon.

"Oh!" said Gretchen with a snap of her fingers. "I almost forgot that toxin will wear off in an hour. By the way Mr. Kane, make sure you wear the suit. See you tonight mein sexy cowboy" she said with a smile and a wave.

She said some words to Scott and Naomi before walking out of the room. Once she was gone Scott grabbed Simon by the back of his shirt and dragged him out of the room followed by Naomi. They walked into an elevator, Naomi pushed a button and the elevator started moving. When the doors opened again, they were in a short hallway. Scott dragged him to a room while Naomi opened the door. He dragged him inside, lifted him up and tossed him on the bed as casually as one might toss unwanted clothes. Once he was on the bed the two of them left and locked the door behind them.

Simon shifted his gaze to his new surroundings. The room was plain with a TV, a bed and a table with two chairs on the other side of the room and the other usual amenities minus a window. On the table was his trench coat which was neatly folded. There was a small room off to the side that Simon assumed was a bathroom. Hanging on a hook on the door was a suit, it consisted of a white dinner jacket with a red corsage, white dress shirt, black tie, black pants and dress shoes.

"What does she think I am? James Bond," thought Simon as he studied the suit.

Eventually, the paralytic began to wear off and he could feel control returning to his limbs. He got out of the bed; his body numb from the toxins. Simon staggered towards the bathroom and was relieved to find it had a shower. Clumsily and weakly he undressed and stepped in the shower and turned on the hot water. He let the water pour over him revitalizing his body. After an hour he felt back to normal and stepped out of the shower and wrapped a towel around his waist.

He saw some hair gel, comb and a toothbrush as well as other amenities that looked familiar on the sink table. He looked in the closet and saw his suitcase inside confirming his suspicions that they stole his, and probably Mai's, things from their hotel room. "Definitely did their homework," he grunted.

He walked over to the suit hanging on the door and studied it. The suit jacket appeared to be by Givenchy which partially irked

Simon as he preferred black dinner jackets by Tom Ford, still it was a nice suit. He was not surprised at how she knew his sizes. Suddenly, there was a knock on the door; Simon tensely approached the door, irritated at his lack of weapons. He opened the door and was both surprised and relieved to see it was Mai, unharmed and most importantly alive. She rushed at him and hugged him, they held each other relieved at finding out they were both safe.

"Come in," said Simon, Mai walked in and sat at the table. Her eyes glanced at the suit then back at Simon as he closed the door.

"I'm glad you're okay" said Mai softly.

"Me too" said Simon as he walked over to the table and sat down.

"Who are these people?" she asked nervously.

"They're called Cobalt Incorporated. Essentially, they're arms dealers" Simon explained.

"I've heard of them. What do they want with us?" asked Mai.

"I'll find out tonight" answered Simon.

Mai raised her eyebrow both confused and at his answer. "Tonight?"

"Yeah...I have a date with their CEO" answered Simon with a shrug.

"A date?" said Mai disbelievingly.

"Yep" said Simon dismissively.

"Right...so what's the plan?" Mai asked.

"Go along with them for now" said Simon.

"That's it?" she asked.

"You got a better idea?" replied Simon sarcastically.

"Well, my room is next to yours" said Mai.

"Good, stay in there I don't trust these people" said Simon sternly.

"Gotcha" said Mai as she stood up to leave, before she walked out the door, she turned to look at Simon. "Good luck on your date" said Mai.

*****

Located on the other side of the world exists Sankan Island. To its inhabitants and the criminal underworld it is commonly known as the Devils Playground. The small city on the island is home to criminals, terrorists and those desperate enough to resort to having to live there. The city is controlled and divided between the Russian Mafia family known as the Vasilev Syndicate and the Chinese Heise She Li Triad. Both organizations maintain headquarters located in two large buildings across the street from one another.

The head of the Triads operations on Sankan, a man known as Deng, sat at his desk both angry and confused in his office. He was a tall relatively young Chinese man dressed in a black suit and tie with a white dress shirt underneath.

Over the last five months he had been assembling a team for Simon Kane to help dismantle the Networc. Now after months of hard work the team was assembled, what vexed him so was that he had been unable to contact him and tell him that they had assembled the team and were ready to begin.

He had instructed the Triads operatives to find him, but his growing impatience gnawed at him like a cancer. Suddenly, he heard a knock on the door of his office.

"It's open," barked Deng, already knowing who it was.

Into the office walked Dengs assistant, a man named Mazin. Deng swiveled his chair around to face him casually. "Well Mazin, what's the word this time?" asked Deng as he leaned back in his chair.

"The word is good...kind of" said Mazin as he sat down in the chair in front of Deng's desk.

"Kind of?" asked Deng as he raised an eyebrow.

"Well we've known where Kane and Mai are, but our problem is that we don't know why we've lost communication with them which means we can't pinpoint there exact location" began Mazin.

"No shit," grunted Deng sarcastically, annoyed at being told what he already knew.

"Yes, well according to what little we were able to find out they were kidnapped" he answered, ignoring Deng's sarcasm.

"Kidnapped, by who, the Networc?" said Deng hoping the answer was no.

"No, by Cobalt Incorporated." Mazin answered.

"Cobalt? The arms dealers? Why the hell would they want Simon and Mai? It makes no sense," said Deng.

"No idea," said Mazin with a shrug. "Maybe we should send the team out there to find them?"

"No, they may have recovered by now, but we don't know the details, besides Simon is resourceful enough to find a way out" said Deng. "Continue investigating I want to know what the hell is going on over there"

"Yes sir" said Mazin as he stood up and exited the office.

Deng spun his chair around and looked out at the city, he felt better knowing why they had been incommunicado but still annoyed at his lack of information.

Chapter 9
.22 Caliber Princess

When Simon finished putting on the suit Gretchen provided him with, he looked at his reflection in the mirror. As he studied his reflection, he couldn't help but feel like James Bond.

"Kane. Simon Kane" said Simon in his best Sean Connery impression before laughing. He had finished slicking his hair backward when he heard a knock on the door. He checked his watch; it read 8:00 pm. He shrugged, walked over to the front door and opened it. Standing in front of him in the doorway was Scott Grant, a surly look on his face.

"Follow me," grunted Scott.

"Whatever you say," said Simon casually, He followed Scott to the elevator at the end of the hallway.

When they arrived at the elevator Scott pushed the button. When the elevator doors opened Simon and Scott walked inside, Scott pressed a button marked penthouse. Once the doors slid shut, they could feel the elevator rise with increasing speed. When the doors opened once again, they were facing the living room of the penthouse. Simon looked around the room. "Damn, I forgot something" said Simon as Scott was about to press the button to close the door.

Scott looked up at him curiously just as Simon spun around and punched him in the nose knocking him to the floor of the elevator. "Never mind I found it." He reached into the elevator and pressed the button for the floor he came from and watched the doors close.

He turned to study the penthouse. It looked obscenely expensive; its walls were painted white. In the middle of the room was a black leather sectional sofa with a wooden coffee table and large flat screen television. Behind the sofa was a door that led to what

Simon assumed was a bedroom. Hanging from the ceiling was an ornate glass chandelier, on the other side of the room were sliding doors that led out to a balcony overlooking Tangier.

"So, this is what arms dealing can buy you," said Simon, as he walked to the sliding doors. He walked onto the balcony and saw a glass table with a candle in the middle, two sets of utensils, plates and empty wine glasses with two chairs.

Simon sat down in one of the chairs and looked out at the city below and the desert beyond. The city glittered in the night sky like lights on a Christmas tree. Suddenly the door slid open, instinctively Simon turned his head around to see who it was. Onto the balcony walked Gretchen wearing a black dress with black heels a diamond necklace and bright red lipstick. Simon had to admit that she did look stunning in the dress since it showed off her seductive hourglass figure. "Enjoying the view?"

"Now I am," said Simon smoothly. She smiled and blushed, her chalk white cheeks getting slightly red. She appeared slightly more relaxed than she did earlier. Simon stood up and pulled out the chair opposite him, she smiled and sat down. Simon returned to his seat casually. "That's quite a dress," he observed flirtatiously.

"Thanks, it's a Versace, are all CIA agents as polite as you?" asked Gretchen.

"Depends, on how you define polite" answered Simon with a sarcastic smirk.

Gretchen laughed softly. "First, I would like to apologize for our…unorthodox method of contacting you. But we couldn't risk you refusing to help us," continued Gretchen.

"Well…of all the times I've been kidnapped this is probably the most enjoyable," said Simon sardonically.

"That's quite a compliment," she replied.

"Would you mind telling me why?" asked Simon.

"Several days ago, we were hired to drive you to Aswan to stop an impending terrorist attack," said Gretchen bluntly.

Simon didn't know what to expect from her, but he was definitely not expecting such an answer. "Well that's a new one, wait, you said drive?"

"Yes why?" answered Gretchen.

"Aswan is on the other side of the continent" said Simon.

"And?" Gretchen replied bluntly.

Simon couldn't help but laugh at her plan. "You must be joking, driving to Aswan from here would take days."

"Three, actually" corrected Gretchen holding up three fingers.

"Why not fly?" Simon asked.

"Because it's safer and under the radar," Gretchen answered.

"It also makes you an easier target," corrected Simon.

"That's what we have you for," said Gretchen. "But in all seriousness, I wouldn't worry about that, we have a plan."

"Right, so who hired you? Why did they want me? And what is this attack to them?" asked Simon.

"Some Israeli security company called Tri-Mark Securities," she answered.

Unlike Gretchen, Simon knew that Tri-Mark Securities was really a front company for Golem. He was curious as to why they had decided to involve themselves in this matter, given the long history of conflict between Egypt and Israel. "I don't know why they wanted you to do it and don't ask me why, I'm just a means to an end," answered Gretchen.

"Aren't we all," grunted Simon.

"Very true, but the real question is who's the means and who is the end" said Gretchen. As she said the words Simon remembered his conversation with Mai earlier when another question occurred to him.

"What about Mai?" asked Simon.

"Oh yes. You're "not" girlfriend. What about her?" asked Gretchen confused.

"How does she fit into this?" he asked.

"She doesn't, we decided to bring her because we believed you would be more compliant if she accompanied you," answered Gretchen.

"I see, and obviously you'll have your goons shoot me and her if we don't go along with this scheme of yours," Simon observed.

"I'd prefer it not come to that….and I prefer not to think of them as goons," said Gretchen with a nod.

"Well, I have one request and it's a deal breaker," said Simon.

"Shoot," said Gretchen curiously as to what it was.

"She comes with us," he answered.

Gretchen was silent for a moment, but Simon could tell she was thinking. "Fine" she said with a smirk.

"And speaking of fine, our food is here," said Gretchen. Simon turned around and saw two waiters, each carrying a covering plate and a drink. Gingerly they placed the plates and drinks on the table in front of them and then left. Gretchen's dinner was fish with red wine, Simon's plate had steak au poivre. It looked and smelled delicious, but what concerned him most was the drink. He smelled the drink and was relieved to find out it was iced tea. "Something wrong?" asked Gretchen as she cut into the fish.

"No, I just wanted to make sure it wasn't alcoholic," said Simon as he picked up his knife and fork.

"Why?" asked Gretchen.

"I don't drink" he answered bluntly.

"That is unusual, a spy that doesn't drink," said Gretchen as Simon began to cut into the steak.

"You watch too many movies," said Simon as he ate a piece of the steak.

"Impossible, you can never watch too many movies," said Gretchen with a smile. "How do you like the steak?"

"It's excellent," he answered. "By the way I'm guessing your twenty-one?"

"Twenty-two actually," she replied with a smile.

"So how does a 22-year-old woman like you become an international arms dealer?" asked Simon.

She grinned. "I didn't get into this business, so much as I was born into it," said Gretchen. "Have you ever heard of Arnold Neubauer?"

"Who hasn't, one of the most infamous arms dealers of his time," answered Simon.

"He was my father. He travelled the world selling guns for years and raising me at the same time," she began. "He taught me everything he knew about the business. When he died, I took over for him," answered Gretchen with a proud smile.

"I remember Time magazine published an article calling him the Caliber King, because of how prolific he was among arms dealers" said Simon.

"That was when I was eight years old. He loved the name so much he started calling me his little caliber princess," said Gretchen with a fond smile.

Simon noticed that her voice was tinged with a hint of grief. "I'm sorry, I lost someone also recently," said Simon.

"Don't worry about it, besides he'd be proud," she replied.

"As I recall, he was the head of a group called Rensler right?" asked Simon.

"Rensler United. We were one of the world's leading arms providers. My father had contacts all over the world and built the company himself, he even worked closely with Gabriel Rojas...though no one could ever prove it" answered Gretchen.

Simon could hear the pride in her voice as she listed her father's accomplishments. But what most surprised him was the mention of Gabriel Rojas.

"Sadly, the company was bought out by Kronos International, broken up and most of its assets were sold to Emperor Eagle Services leaving my family with nothing," continued Gretchen. "Naturally they offered me a job, but I refused"

"So rather than join the people that stole your father's legacy, you went out on your own, using his old contacts, to establish Cobalt Inc" inferred Simon.

"Exactly Mr. Kane," said Gretchen.

"Nice to know you're following in his footsteps" said Simon sardonically.

"Like I said, he would be proud" replied Gretchen. "I'm sure the CIA had countless, files on him."

"Before my time," said Simon dismissively. In truth while he knew little about Kronos International, he knew a great deal about Emperor Eagle Services. The CIA relied on Rensler United for its own operations while Emperor Eagle had always been Silhouettes preferred ally. As a result, while both were unaware of who they were really working for, an intense rivalry had developed between the two. Simon assumed that when Rensler was bought out that the rivalry was over. However, he was surprised to find out that this was the reason for the bitter rivalry that existed between Emperor Eagle and Cobalt.

"And what about the two goons?" asked Simon.

"Well, after I established Cobalt, I needed bodyguards, so I recruited them after they left the Royal Marines," answered Gretchen. "And that's my story."

"Hell of a story" said Simon as he drank some of his iced tea.

"What about you?" asked Gretchen. "I read your file but there are some gaps in it that were blacked out and I love a good mystery, like that eye patch, for example, what happened?"

"I slipped in the shower" said Simon dryly.

Gretchen looked at him and suddenly laughed. "Slipped in the shower, that's rich seriously, though how did it happen?"

"I lost it on a mission," said Simon bluntly. He decided to change the subject. "When do we leave for Aswan?"

"Tomorrow morning…in a gun truck," answered Gretchen.

Of course, she has a damn gun truck. "And where is the gun truck?" asked Simon.

"In our warehouse at the harbor," Gretchen answered.

"Well then, here's to a safe journey," said Simon as he raised his glass.

"I'll drink to that," said Gretchen as they toasted their glasses and took a drink. The waiters returned and took their empty silverware, glasses and plates away.

"So, Mr. Kane I take it you enjoyed your dinner?" said Gretchen.

"Considerably," said Simon.

"Would you care to join me in my room for some dessert?" asked Gretchen with an amorous smile.

"I've never been one to turn down dessert," said Simon with a knowing smirk.

"Neither have I," said Gretchen coquettishly as she stood up.

Simon followed her inside and into the penthouses master bedroom. It was a large ornate room with a red carpet and light brown walls. In the middle was the bed and on the other side a dresser with a large mirror. Upon entering the room, Simon closed the door behind him casually. As he turned around to face Gretchen, she walked up to him. Before he could respond she wrapped her arms around him and kissed him on the lips.

"A little forward, aren't you?" he asked slyly as he put his hands gently on her hips.

"I don't like to waste time," whispered Gretchen seductively as her lips moved closer to his.

"Always liked German efficiency" said Simon as they kissed each other.

Simon unzipped the back of her dress as Gretchen slid off his dinner jacket. Gretchen backed away and motioned to Simon to follow her before turning around; she began to remove her bra and got on the bed. When she turned around Simon noticed a large tattoo of a blue Chinese dragon running down the left side of her back. "Some tattoo," observed Simon.

"I'm glad you like it," said Gretchen.

"I bet there's a story behind it," Simon replied smoothly as he quickly undressed and climbed into bed next to Gretchen.

"Why don't you let me tell you?" suggested Gretchen amorously In seconds they were both naked. Simon ran his fingers through her hair and onto the soft skin of her back. He kissed her on the neck causing her to sigh with pleasure. Gretchen gently rubbed his back with her hands as they lay down in the bed passionately making love until they eventually fell asleep in each other's arms.

Chapter 10
The Cobalt Express

The sun had yet to rise over Tangier, thus the harbor was enveloped in the darkness and desolation of the early morning. Scott, Naomi and Mai were the first to arrive at the Cobalt warehouse.

It was a large dilapidated building surrounded by other warehouses in the harbor. On the front of the warehouse was the faded Cobalt Incorporated logo. Having been rousted from sleep at five in the morning, Mai was asleep in the car while Scott and Naomi were outside drinking coffee.

"How's the nose?" asked Naomi thoughtfully, after taking a sip of her coffee.

"Better now. I swear I'm going to shove that yanks head so far up his ass it'll come out his neck," Scott grunted.

"Graphic as ever luv," said Naomi quietly. "Still, I'd be careful, I think Gretchen likes him."

"Good for him," he grumbled before taking a sip of his coffee.

"Don't worry I still love you despite your busted nose" said Naomi with a warm smile.

"Thanks, luv, when're they supposed to get here anyway?" Scott asked.

Naomi checked her watch. "Ten minutes ago," she answered, sounding mildly annoyed.

"Bloody hell" grumbled Scott. "So you think this is just another of Gretchen's flings like the time with that Russian woman or if it's permanent?"

Naomi shrugged her shoulders, "who knows? I gave up trying to predict Gretchen years ago." They both looked at each other and could tell what the other was thinking.

"It's a fling," said Scott and Naomi at the same time.

Suddenly, they heard a car approaching, "about bloody time," barked Scott.

"Mai! Wake up!" yelled Naomi as she tapped the car window.

Mai jumped at the sudden awakening and then groggily exited the car. Gretchen parked next to Naomi and Scotts' car. "Good Morning!" said Gretchen cheerfully as she got out of the car.

Gretchen was wearing her white blazer with her black dress shirt and red tie underneath with a white skirt and black heels. Simon followed her out of the car, he was dressed in his dark blue trench coat, green pants and black dress shirt, feeling nowhere near as awake as Gretchen despite the coffee in his hand.

"Is that really the right attire for this sort of thing?" asked Mai upon seeing Gretchen. "It is for a business meeting," she answered quickly.

Scott walked up to Simon once he was out of the car. "So how's the nose?" asked Simon smugly as he took a sip of coffee.

Scott glared at him angrily. "Screw you, that's how it is"

"So…. not good then," said Simon with a smirk.

"At least I can see out of both eyes," replied Scott.

"And yet you still couldn't see that punch coming," Simon quipped. Scott shrugged, unable to think of a clever comeback.

"Now then," said Gretchen as she clapped her hands together in an attempt to get everything back on track. "Are we ready to go or are we ready to go?"

"What kind of question is that?" said Mai as she put on her glasses.

Gretchen glanced at her with a look of confusion. "Either we're ready to go or we're not ready to go,"

Naomi leaned over to Mai before she could react. "Just go with it," she whispered. Mai shrugged and adjusted her glasses.

"We're ready, everything's inside," said Scott gesturing to the warehouse.

"Lead the way," said Gretchen.

Simon and Gretchen followed Naomi, Mai and Scott into the warehouse.

"So…Simon how did you sleep?" asked Mai while Naomi and Scott unlocked the massive sliding doors of the warehouse.

"Oh, I wouldn't say there was a lot of sleeping" purred Gretchen before Simon could answer.

Mai looked at Simon inquisitively. "What does she mean by that?"

"Don't worry about it," answered Simon dismissively. Before Mai could reply, Naomi and Scott slid open the massive steel doors of the warehouse. The inside was pitch black though Simon caught a few glints of metal but couldn't see inside clearly. Simon, Mai and Gretchen followed Scott and Naomi inside. Naomi flipped several switches on the wall and the warehouse was illuminated. It was mostly desolate inside except for the giant black M939 gun truck in the middle. Against the wall was a table with various guns on it.

The gun truck consisted of a cab in the front. The back was essentially a giant roofless black box with two Browning M37 mounted machine gun's on the left and right sides. The entire truck was armored as much as possible.

Simon hadn't seen a gun truck since his time in Iraq, he whistled at the sight of it.

"How the hell did you get these?" asked Simon.

Gretchen placed her hands on his shoulder, "I have my ways Mein sexy cowboy."

"What?" asked Mai curiously while Simon pinched the bridge of his nose

"Oi, can we get down to business" interrupted Scott, standing at the table holding an L86A2 SA80 assault rifle.

"You heard the man," grunted Simon welcoming the interruption.

Naomi walked up to Simon, holding a gun and holster in her left hand and a bracelet in her right hand. "I believe these are yours" she said as she handed his Jericho, still in its holster, and wrist blade to him.

"I was wondering where they went" said Simon as he removed his trench coat and put it on the table. He took the holster and slid his arms through the holster's loops.

"I never figured you for the bracelet type," Naomi mused as Simon clasped the bracelet, containing the wrist blade, around his left wrist.

"Well, you know what they say get the right tool for the right job," quipped Simon as he flicked his wrist back and the blade popped out.

"Clever little gadget" Naomi remarked.

"It has its uses" said Simon dryly as he put on his trench coat back. He shifted his attention to the table and scanned it. Lying on the end of the table was a familiar looking rifle. It was a Heckler and Koch 416 assault rifle. Simon picked it up and studied the rifle, it was a metallic grey with an ACOG scope and a shoulder strap.

"Quite a gun isn't it?" said Naomi.

"Yeah, it's a hell of a gun," Simon replied dismissively as he slung it over his shoulder.

"Personally, I prefer the H&K G3," said Naomi as she lifted the rifle off the table and slung it over her shoulder.

"Too each his own," said Simon dryly as he did the same. "What about gas?" he asked pointing at the truck.

"Don't worry there's plenty of spare gas in the back," said Scott as he stood behind one of the Browning's.

"And if that's not enough there's also solar panels on the roof and sides in case we run out," finished Gretchen.

"Nice to know you've thought of everything" he said dryly.

"I always do," replied Gretchen with that large grin of hers.

"So, we ready to go?" asked Simon.

"You know it," said Gretchen's voice from the cab.

"Mai, stay with me," said Simon gruffly. Mai shrugged, looking annoyed at having orders barked at her.

"Fine, I guess you're driving Naomi," said Gretchen.

Naomi climbed into the cab while Mai and Simon climbed into the back. Leaning against the walls of the back of the truck were Scott and Naomi's rifles. Simon placed his H&K next to them. Mai sat on the floor and leaned against the wall. Simon got behind the Browning on the right and checked it. Naomi turned the key and the truck roared to life.

Once they were out of the warehouse Naomi and Scott got out and closed the doors. Simon looked down at Mai and saw that she was already fast asleep. He took off his trench coat and covered Mai with it. While Scott and Naomi slid the doors shut and locked them. Scott got in the back and stood behind the other Browning as Naomi got back in the cab.

"Wait! Before we go, I can't believe I forgot," said Gretchen just as Naomi was about to shift into first gear.

"What?" asked Naomi, Gretchen quickly pulled out her phone, plugged it into the radio, turned up the volume and pressed play.

Suddenly the truck began blasting out loud music. "Love that song" said Scott.

"It's Mean Machine by U.D.O," answered Gretchen nonchalantly.

The truck lurched forward and began to slowly pick up speed. Simon looked down at Mai relieved that she was still asleep. At that moment, on a rooftop across the street from them was Counselor Cathcart. He was watching them with a pair of binoculars like a hunter studying his prey. As they disappeared into the horizon, he returned his binoculars to his pocket and pulled out a cellphone. Quickly he dialed a heavily encrypted number. Within minutes, he was greeted by the scrambled voice of Mr. Zero.

"Mr. Zero, Kane is on the move," said Counselor Cathcart.

"Understood, we're tracking them now," replied Mr. Zero.

"What do you want me to do?" asked Counselor Cathcart, silently hoping he would say kill them, so he could avenge Counselor Black.

"Your mission has changed, proceed to Project: Moses in Aswan," said Mr. Zero. "The Lower Echelon will handle Simon Kane," said Mr. Zero, before hanging up abruptly.

"Dammit" muttered Counselor Cathcart as he returned the phone to his pocket.

He had been looking forward to killing Simon Kane, as revenge for Counselor Black. For years Counselor Black and Counselor Cathcart worked side by side. He cursed himself for being too sick to help him with Project: Big Picture. He always thought that if he was there Counselor Black would still be alive and the plan would have succeeded. But it didn't matter now, he had new orders and had to follow them.

Chapter 11
Through Hells Creation

The bright orange sand dunes of the Sahara Desert seemed to go on forever. In the hours that they had been driving, the dark morning sky had slowly changed to the light blue of the early afternoon. Simon wiped the sweat from his forehead and looked out at the endless sandy infinite and wondered how anything could live in such an unforgiving place. The road was empty save for the occasional car or animal carcass. From above beams of heat rained down on them from the sun.

He glanced downward at Mai, she was still asleep on the floor curled up in his trench coat.

"So, what's the deal with you two anyway?" asked Scott.

Simon shifted his attention to Scott who was leaning against the edge of the truck. "It's complicated," answered Simon.

"What isn't?" grunted Scott. The two men were quiet for a minute as they scanned the horizon.

"So, how long were you two with the Royal Marines," asked Simon.

"Five years, what about you," replied Scott.

"SEALs for two years, then five with the agency," answered Simon.

"That explains why you hit so bloody hard then," replied Scott.

"Yeah, sorry about that," said Simon.

"Forget it mate. We can have a rematch later," said Scott. "I understand why though, if some sod laid a hand on Naomi, I'd break a few bones myself."

"I'm glad we can agree on that, speaking of which how long have you two been married," asked Simon.

Scott smiled as he glanced at the ring. "Three years, you got someone?"

"Used to," answered Simon quietly as he thought about Sheila.

"Sorry to hear that," said Scott.

"It's alright, she's in a better place now," he replied. Simon thought about Scott and Naomi and couldn't help but be reminded of how devoted he and Sheila were to each other. He decided it best to change the subject. "I've been wondering about something though."

"What?" asked Scott.

"How exactly did you two end up working for a certifiable arms dealer? Gretchen told me the basics, but I wouldn't mind knowing the details," asked Simon.

"Yeah, Gretchen's a piece of work, isn't she?" said Scott with a laugh.

"That's putting it mildly," replied Simon.

"Well it's quite a story, we met in the Royal Marines and fell for each other. After we got out of the service, we intended to get married," said Scott. "However, my parents objected to me marrying Naomi because of her Jamaican heritage."

"It's crazy isn't it, their son goes to war, meets the love of his life and wants to get married. Yet, they object to it because his fiancé's black of all the bloody things," said Scott.

"It's more terrible than crazy I'd say, so what happened next" asked Simon.

"Well, after telling my parents to go to hell we managed to save up and have a small wedding," said Scott. "However, we were almost broke, so after three months of working at every fast food joint you yanks exported to us, we were offered the job by Gretchen and lacking any other choice we accepted it," said Scott. "Besides we both kind of missed the adventure of it all."

"That's quite a story, it'd make a hell of a movie," said Simon.

"Too right mate, I could totally see myself being played by that Statham guy." said Scott.

"Do you know why she hired you two?" asked Simon.

"Mate, I gave up trying to figure that bird out a long time ago," answered Scott. He shrugged, "Naomi asked her once and she said it was because we're a cute couple."

Suddenly Simon heard a noise approaching from behind them. "You hear that?" he asked quickly.

Scott listened intently. "Yeah, sounds like a motorcycle."

"I was afraid of that," said Simon.

"Here use these" said Scott as he tossed a pair of binoculars at Simon. He caught them and looked in the direction of the noise. He zoomed in and saw a helmeted man on a rapidly approaching yellow motorcycle. He was about to look away, dismissing it as just another tourist, when the driver reached into a compartment of the bike and pulled out a submachine gun.

"Oh shit, get down!" yelled Simon just as the man opened fire. Simon and Scott jumped to the ground narrowly avoiding being hit. Mai woke up, awakened by the gunfire.

"What's going on?" yelled Mai.

"Road rage," grunted Simon as he drew his pistol. In the cabin Naomi and Gretchen knelt their heads down as the driver shot their windows as he drove past them.

"I knew bulletproof windows would come in handy" said Gretchen with a smile as she looked up at the cracked but still intact passenger window. The truck swerved wildly but Naomi stabilized it. The motorcyclist drove ahead of them stopped and turned around as he quickly reloaded his SMG. Simon jumped up and fired three rounds at the motorcyclist with his pistol. The bullets hit him in the back, and he fell down on the road.

Naomi slowed down and they all disembarked from the truck. Naomi, Scott, Gretchen and Mai looked for any signs of damage. Simon walked over to the body of the man, pistol in hand. The man was gasping for breath as blood spilled from his mouth. "You may have killed me but the Networc will send more Mr. Kane you will never make it to Aswan," gasped the man through blood-stained teeth.

Simon stopped in his tracks at the mention of the Networc. For the first time in months he had encountered an operative of the sinister conclave that murdered Sheila. Simon grabbed him by the jacket excitedly. "Who controls the Networc?" he demanded.

The dying man grinned smugly. "Mr. Zero......you'll never find him," said the man as he breathed his last.

Simon stood there confused at his cryptic last words. He searched the man for anything that could be used as a clue to find the Networc, but he found nothing. He walked back to the truck, his mind racing with more questions than answers. The dominant question being: who is Mr. Zero? As he approached the others, they could tell that Simon had heard something from the man by the look on his face.

"How's the truck?" asked Simon.

"Fine, just a couple dents," replied Scott.

"Good, because we need to move now," said Simon.

"What did that guy say to you?" asked Gretchen. Simon knew she would not take no for an answer.

"More guys like him are going to come after us," said Simon.

"Who are they?" asked Naomi,

Simon didn't know how to explain it since there was so much, he didn't know. "They're called the Networc, I've had run-ins with them before. All I know about them is that they are extremely dangerous."

"They have an army of highly-trained well-armed mercenaries and if they want us dead, we are dead" said Simon warily.

They were all quiet for several minutes looking at each other processing what Simon said.

"Well gang I think you know what we have to do" said Gretchen quietly. Naomi and Scott nodded and got in the truck. Mai and Simon felt like they were missing something. Scott and Mai got in the back of the truck. Gretchen got in the passenger seat next to Naomi.

"Want to tell me what we're doing exactly," asked Simon. Gretchen looked up from her phone and looked directly at Simon, an unsettling grin creeping across her face.

"Cowboy, this isn't the first time someone's tried to kill us, we know what to do," replied Gretchen.

"Which is?" asked Mai.

"Take care of business," said Gretchen. Simon and Mai looked at each other, they shrugged and got in the back of the truck. Once they were inside Naomi started the engine, and the truck began to move forward.

"Pump up the Kenny Loggins cuz we're heading into the Danger Zone bitches," said Gretchen as she pushed a button on her phone.

Suddenly the radio started playing Danger Zone by Kenny Loggins at full volume. Simon, Mai and Scott could hear the radio in the back. "So, her solution is Kenny Loggins?" asked Mai.

"Could be worse" said Simon.

Mai looked at him confused. "How, how could this possibly be worse?"

"She could be playing Nirvana," said Simon.

The three of them laughed at the joke as the truck rolled forward into hells creation.

Chapter 12
Pieces On A Chessboard

Mr. One entered his office and sat down at his desk casually located on the top floor of the Applied Dynamics building in Johannesburg, South Africa. Adorning the walls were heads of animals he had shot while on safari. Among them were lions, rhinos and a few zebras. He would often look up at the heads and feel a sense of pride. Today, however, he felt nervous and afraid as he awaited a phone call. He leaned back in his chair and sighed.

Mr. One reached into his desk and pulled out a bottle of Tanzanian red wine and a shot glass. He sighed in relief at the temporary relief the drink would afford him as he poured the wine into the glass. Suddenly his phone began to ring, he stopped knowing full well who it was. He quickly pulled the phone from his pocket and answered it. "Mr. One, this is Mr. Zero," said the voice on the other end of the phone.

His face went white with fear as he heard the words. He gulped nervously, Mr. Zero never called unless something was wrong or if he needed anything. "Yes sir."

"Mr. One, I've been monitoring your man's progress against Simon Kane" said Mr. Zero, his voice reduced to a crackly static whisper over the scrambled phone call.

"Is something wrong?" asked Mr. One.

"He failed, did you actually think one man with a motorcycle and a gun would be able to take down five people in a gun truck?" asked Mr. Zero.

Mr. One stammered. "Sir, I figured that a lightning fast attack would be the most effective."

"You figured wrong, I've been watching the feed from his helmet camera, he's dead," replied Mr. Zero. "But what is more troubling to me is what he said to Simon Kane"

"What did he say?" asked Mr. One.

"He told him my name. Specifically, my codename," said Mr. Zero.

"Sir, with all due respect, it is highly doubtful Kane will ever be able to trace that name back to you. Hell, no one ever has" protested Mr. One.

"That goes without saying, my question is why did he say that in the first place?" Mr. Zero inquired.

"Sir, he probably believed that it would throw Kane off his game, make him doubt himself," Mr. One replied trying not to sound nervous.

The phone was quiet for several seconds. Mr. One wondered what Mr. Zero was thinking, and what he was going to say next. "I see, so its psychological warfare then?"

"Yes sir," answered Mr. One.

"A clever strategy, how do you intend to take him and his associates down this time?" asked Mr. Zero.

Mr. One cleared his throat. "Well sir, since our first attempt failed, we're going to try a more direct approach using predator drones," he answered, feeling confident that Mr. Zero would commend him for it.

"That would draw too much attention from the Algerians. Deploy the Lower Echelon's ground forces instead," answered Mr. Zero.

"Understood sir, I will handle it" said Mr. One, masking his irritation at having his plan picked apart.

"See that you do," Mr. Zero replied, before hanging up the phone.

Mr. One returned the phone to his pocket and took a deep breath relieved that the call was over. He shifted his attention to the glass of wine on his desk. He drank the glass dry in one gulp, then he looked at his computer. On the screen was a satellite map of the Sahara tracking Kane's crew across it in real time. They were in the middle of the Algerian desert; he leaned over his computer and typed a message on his computer reading:

Primary blackout maneuver has failed, intercept and terminate Cobalt Incorporated convoy before it reaches Aswan in Egypt, kill everyone in the convoy, targets are heavily armed.

Upon completing the message, he quickly reread it. He then sent the message to the base commander of an Applied Dynamics compound outside Algiers. His task accomplished, he sighed with relief and poured himself another glass of wine.

*****

The United Egyptian Front consisted of ten men each of them a veteran of the Egyptian Special Forces. They were all stone faced; rough men disillusioned by recent events in their country. They sat in their warehouse headquarters in Aswan waiting. Their leader, a tall angry looking man referred to by his men only as General Faisel checked his watch.

"Where is he?" Faisel grunted, referring to the mysterious man who had assembled them in the first place.

As if in answer the front door of the building opened, standing in the doorway was their enigmatic benefactor. "It's about time Cathcart," said Faisel, impatient and annoyed.

"General, general, we've been over this, it's Counselor Cathcart," he replied smugly as he walked into the room.

"Counselor of what," said one of the men with a smirk. "You don't want to know," replied the Counselor dismissively.

"Gentlemen, is everything going according to plan so far," asked Cathcart.

"Yes, all we are waiting for is the right moment," said General Faisel.

"Good, because the moment is fast approaching," replied Counselor Cathcart.

"Why do we need him to do this?" barked one of the soldiers.

Cathcart looked at the mouthy soldier smugly, "because I have the arming codes for the bomb,"

"Then give them to us now" growled the soldier.

Cathcart smiled. "Why don't you take it from me little man?" Furiously the soldier leaped at Cathcart. Before he could lay a hand on him, Cathcart calmly stepped to the side. Bewildered and furious, the soldier landed on the hard cement floor face down with a barely audible thud. Before the soldier could get up Cathcart jammed his foot onto the man's neck roughly. He pulled a silenced Glock 19 out of his shoulder holster, aimed it at the back of the man's head and fired it. He could sense the other soldiers approaching from behind, he swung around and aimed the pistol at them. "Make no mistake all of you. I'm not working for you, you are working for me."

They backed away like frightened animals though Cathcart could see the contempt for him in their eyes. Cathcart holstered the pistol and shifted his attention to Faisel. "General, get control of your men,"

Faisel nodded in response. Cathcart turned to leave, as he opened the door, he looked back at the now nine members of the UEF. "The next time we meet, will be at the Dam so get ready."

"And, by the way clean that shit up," said Cathcart gesturing to the dead body on the floor closing the door behind him.

Chapter 13
Sunset Riders

They had been driving for hours through the desert without incident. The sun was beginning to set turning the light blue sky darker and the white wisps of cloud into bright yellow and orange streaks that looked like cotton candy. Stars were beginning to appear in the evening sky. The dwindling light from the sun bounced off the sea of sand dunes slowly turning the brown dunes into smooth black hills that seemed to stretch on forever. Ahead of them the road stretched onward, a lonely marker of civilization in a lifeless wasteland.

Gretchen sat next to Naomi writing in her notebook while Naomi sat next to her driving. "What's a better name: the War Wagon or the Cobalt Express?"

Naomi looked at her somewhat confused. "Better name for what?"

"I'm trying to come up with a cool name for this truck, so far I've managed to narrow it down to either the Cobalt Express or the War Wagon" explained Gretchen.

"Why name it at all?" asked Naomi.

"Because I'm thinking of buying it from Tri-Mark Securities when this is over" answered Gretchen casually.

"What makes you think they'll sell it to you?" asked Naomi half serious.

Gretchen looked up from her notebook and looked at Naomi, a serious look on her face. "Because if there's one thing my father taught me it's that everything and anyone has a price, the only question is how much."

"My father taught me recipes," replied Naomi with a shrug.

"Very nice, anything good?" replied Gretchen.

"Mostly Jamaican recipes so yes," replied Naomi. "What other names do you have?"

"The Thunder Wagon, The Meat Wagon, The Imperator, The Gretchen Mobile et cetera" answered Gretchen dismissively.

"The Gretchen mobile?" replied Naomi skeptically.

"Yeah you know like the Batmobile?" she replied.

The two laughed heartily at the cheesiness of the name. When they had finished Naomi yawned quietly. "You alright? You've been driving all day," asked Gretchen.

"Nothing, just tired" said Naomi.

"Pull over," said Gretchen.

Naomi shrugged and pulled the truck over to the side of the desolate road. Gretchen leaned her head out the window and yelled "Scott! Take over driving."

In the back, Scott was manning one of the Browning's while Simon was sitting on the floor next to Mai. "Have fun," said Simon sarcastically, as Scott disembarked from the back of the truck.

When Scott and Naomi walked past each other they gave each other a high-five. Naomi sat down across from Simon and Mai. Within seconds the truck started moving again. Having slept all day Mai wasn't feeling sleepy and was somewhat glad to have another woman to talk to. "Y'know, I'm not tired at all I could drive it," said Mai.

"Thanks, but I don't think this rig is the kind of vehicle you're used to," said Naomi politely.

"I wouldn't doubt her too much, she managed to drive through Sankan City while being chased by every goon on the island," explained Simon.

"Sankan? You too have been to Sankan?" asked Naomi incredulously.

"Unfortunately, yes" said Mai with a shrug.

"I've heard rumors about Sankan, but I've never actually been there," responded Naomi.

Simon looked at her mildly surprised. "Why? I would think that would be a paradise for an arms dealer like Gretchen, she only goes there if she has to since it has a bad history for her,"

"You'd think but the Triad refuses to allow arms dealers on the island for some reason.... except Gretchen" explained Naomi.

"The Triad has a distrust of arms dealers but if they prove themself worthy they are given a mark that allows them to operate there," Mai explained. *That explains the tattoo,* thought Simon.

"How do you know that?" asked Naomi curiously.

Mai sighed. "My father is the leader of the Heise She Li Triad."

"Didn't see that coming," said Naomi surprised. "So...how'd you end up here with this yank?" she asked gesturing to Simon with her thumb.

"It's a long story," said Simon.

"I like long stories, they usually have the best endings," Naomi replied with a smile.

They grinned at the joke. "In my case I hope so," said Mai.

"Six months ago, I was kidnapped by the Rojas Cartel and taken to Sankan Island since they were at war with Syndicate and the Triad" began Mai. "So, my father hired Simon to rescue me from the cartel and to act as my bodyguard for the next six months."

"Quite a story," said Naomi dryly.

"You don't know the half of it," said Simon sardonically.

"I'll bet, there's always more to every story," Naomi said quietly.

As they talked the sun had begun to sink lower and lower taking the light with it. The stars and moon were more visible and brighter. The darkness of night had rendered the surrounding desert invisible.

"I never noticed how beautiful the stars are. In China, the pollution is so thick you can't even see the sky, but out here it's so beautiful," said Mai as she looked up at the sky studying the stars. Naomi and Simon glanced upward as well.

"It sure is," said Simon.

"Peaceful too," agreed Naomi.

"It's funny. Whenever I see stars like this I'm always reminded of my mother," said Mai quietly.

Simon and Naomi looked at her curiously, "She used to have a diamond necklace that looked just like them" said Mai. "She wore it everywhere she went, even on the day she was killed."

"I'm sorry," said Naomi gently.

"It's fine, besides they don't remind me of losing her, they remind me of her," said Mai gently. Simon thought about what she said and looked at the stars, he didn't know if it was what Mai was saying but he couldn't help but think of Sheila. He wondered, was she looking down at him from up above, missing him as much as he missed her. Naomi could tell that Mai's words resonated with him.

"You lost someone, too didn't you?" said Naomi.

Simon looked back at Naomi. "Haven't we all?"

She shrugged in response. "I'll see you two in the morning," said Naomi as she lay down and began to fall asleep.

As they drove on through the night Simon and Mai began to drift off into sleep themselves.

Chapter 14
Wacky Racers

Mai was the first to hear it, the noise rousted her from sleep. It sounded distant but was quickly getting closer. She stood up and instinctively covered her eyes from the bright morning sunlight. Once her eyes had adjusted to the light, she looked around and saw nothing new. She listened closely for the noise to try and pinpoint where it was coming from and more importantly what it was.

It sounded like a million flies buzzing all at once through a microphone and that ominous noise was getting louder. She looked to her left and saw two small black dots on the horizon getting closer, she squinted to try and make it out, but she couldn't identify the source of the noise. She rubbed her eyes and put on her glasses hoping that they would at least make the dots easier to identify. She squinted and the dots now looked like small helicopters.

"What the hell?" muttered Mai as she tried to figure out what helicopters were doing out here in the desert.

Her thoughts were interrupted by a salvo of bullets hitting the side of the truck coming from the helicopters. Instinctively, Mai ducked behind the trucks protective armored walls. The loud clanging of metal colliding with metal woke Naomi and Simon up immediately.

"Dammit!" yelled Simon.

In the cab the scene was the same, Gretchen was rousted from sleep by the attacking helicopters. The lead helicopter flew low over the truck while the other one followed behind it. Simon and Naomi immediately recognized the choppers as AH-6 Little Bird helicopters with M249 SAW heavy machine guns on the left and right of the pilot. Simon and Naomi each got behind a

Browning and aimed them at the attacking Little Birds.

"Mai keep your head down!" yelled Simon as they cocked the Brownings. The helicopters turned around to face the side of the truck. They came in from the left inundating the gun truck with machine gun fire. The choppers flew closer and closer as Gretchen pulled a snub-nosed Smith and Wesson 642 revolver out of her pocket. As the helicopters flew overhead, Gretchen leaned out of the side window and began firing at the tail of one of the helicopters.

"Goddamnit! I was sleeping you schweinhunds!" yelled Gretchen as she fired at the helicopters. The helicopters turned back around as the gun stopped firing and started clicking.

"Scheisse" muttered Gretchen as she realized she was out of ammo. She quickly ejected the spent shells from her revolver and pulled a speed reloader, with five bullets in it, out of her pocket.

"It's been a while since you've had to use that," said Scott dryly as Gretchen slid each bullet into a chamber.

"Why would I have to use it when I have you two?" observed Gretchen as she pulled back the revolvers hammer. Simon and Naomi began firing at the helicopters while Mai crouched down and covered her head for safety. Scott swerved the truck from left to right to minimize the chances of getting hit.

"Dammit they're too fast!" yelled Naomi. The helicopters swerved out of the way of the machine gun fire and resumed firing. Simon and Naomi ducked behind the trucks armored walls. The helicopters flew over them again unleashing another lead salvo. Simon and Naomi knelt down in an attempt to avoid getting hit. "We can't take another hit like that," she barked.

"No shit," grunted Simon as he stood up and manned his Browning.

The helicopters turned around for another pass, this time from the left side of the truck. Simon centered the Browning on the lead helicopter and depressed the trigger. Heavy caliber bullets tore through the glass window on the front of the helicopter. The copter started to list back and forth before finally crashing nose first into the sand and exploding. The other helicopter flew over them ignoring its destroyed comrade.

Seizing her opportunity Naomi manned the Browning on the right side, however when she centered it on the copter's cockpit it swerved out of the way towards the front of the truck. Naomi pulled the trigger and followed the chopper with her Browning. Her bullets shredded the tail of the helicopter causing it to lose stability and altitude. It began to list towards the front of the truck. Scott taking advantage of the chopper descending in front of him jammed his foot on the gas. "Hold on lads!" he yelled.

"He isn't," said Simon.

"He is," Naomi replied bluntly.

Gretchen instinctively ducked under the dashboard. Before anyone could react, the truck slammed into the nose of the faltering chopper knocking it aside into the desert. The impact shook the truck almost knocking Simon and Naomi onto the floor. Remarkably, the truck was still intact and continued moving forward. Behind them the helicopter spun in circles before finally crashing onto the road and exploding in a rolling fireball of flame and twisted metal.

"That's my Scott," said Naomi with a smile as she raised her head.

"Damn," said Gretchen as she stuck her head out of the window watching the chopper roll behind them.

"What just happened?" asked Mai feeling shaken.

"We just ran over a helicopter," said Simon as he regained his footing.

"Never a dull moment is there?" muttered Mai sarcastically.

Simon looked down and saw that Mai had a bloody nose. She must have fallen during the impact thought Simon. "Your nose is bleeding," she said.

"What?" said Mai as she noticed the fresh bloodspots on her leg.

She quickly pulled a cloth out of her pocket and wiped the blood off her face, feeling embarrassed. Out of the corner of his eye Simon noticed her glasses on the floor. Gingerly he picked them up and handed them to her.

"I recommend contacts" said Simon with a smile. Mai removed the cloth from her nose and took the glasses. "You alright?"

Mai nodded feeling slightly better as she affixed her glasses. "Good to know."

Simon turned his focus to Naomi. "You alright?"

"Yeah" grunted Naomi.

Suddenly he stood up and spun around quickly, a thought occurring to him. "Shit, what about Gretchen and Scott?" barked Simon nervously.

"Don't worry we're fine," yelled Gretchen from the cabin as if in answer.

"We need to stop and check the truck!" Simon yelled.

"Hell no! We have a schedule," Gretchen barked.

"Well so much for that," muttered Simon.

"Were you expecting a different answer, we're on a schedule," said Naomi dryly.

"Yeah and God forbid we get there late" Simon grunted.

****

Watching them via satellite was Mr. One. Slowly his rage built until he couldn't restrain it any longer. Furiously, he slammed his fist down on his desk.

"Dammit" growled Mr. One as he watched the truck slowly creep across his computer screen.

He focused on his next move thinking carefully. He knew Mr. Zero was watching this and was aware of these developments as well as the current status of Project: MOSES.

As far as Mr. One knew, Counselor Cathcart was handling that matter in Egypt. If Kane managed to interfere with Project: MOSES like he did with Project: BIG PICTURE, there would be hell to pay, thought Mr. One. Still, he was confident that he would not end up like the late Mr. Four who had been executed by Counselor Black for failure and replaced. He shuddered nervously at the thought of being visited by a Counselor. But that would never happen even if Project: MOSES failed the Networc would be able to recover from it, thought Mr. One.

Chapter 15
Riders On The Storm

Night had fallen on the Sahara, the only light that was visible was the truck as it rolled along the desert road. Mai was asleep against the walls of the truck oblivious to its shaking. Simon stood at the back his arms resting on the back wall looking out at the desert. While his eyes studied the shifting terrain, his mind was focused on Sheila. Seeing Naomi and Scott reminded him of their time together. "I know that look in your eyes, who are you thinking about?" she asked innocently.

Simon looked over at her, his thoughts interrupted. "An old friend."

"I overheard parts of your conversation with Scott," said Naomi.

"And?" said Simon.

"Well for what it's worth, I'm sorry for your loss," Naomi replied warmly.

"Thanks. Her name was Sheila," said Simon.

"Were you two in the SEAL's together?" continued Naomi.

Simon grinned. "No, she was ex-Delta Force, we met in the Agency."

"So, what's going on between you two?" said Naomi gesturing to Mai. She was asleep on the floor, using Simon's trench coat as protection from the cool night winds of the desert.

"I don't know what you're talking about," said Simon feigning ignorance.

"C'mon, I'm not blind mate. I've seen the way you two are with each other," said Naomi smugly. Simon knew he was caught, so he sighed frustrated.

"You two have been together for so long you've developed feelings for each other," said Naomi.

"It doesn't matter whether we have or haven't," said Simon wearily.

"How?" Naomi asked confused.

"Because I'm not going to let what happened to Sheila happen to her," said Simon bluntly.

"You can't be sure that Mai will end up like she did" Naomi remarked.

"I also can't be sure that she won't," countered Simon sternly.

"Or in other words you're afraid to get close to someone because you're afraid to lose them," said Naomi.

"Basically," Simon replied dryly.

"Right then so what about the other night with Gretchen?" asked Naomi. Simon was equally surprised and nervous to hear that she knew that.

"How did you?" asked Simon.

"Our room is in the penthouse also," interrupted Naomi.

"Oh," grunted Simon.

"So, what was that then?" asked Naomi.

"One hell of a night," said Simon with a cocky grin.

Naomi laughed. "It certainly sounded like one."

"Still I wouldn't worry about having any problems with Scott and me regarding your "after dinner" romp with Gretchen", said Naomi. "Who she sleeps with is none of our concern."

Before Simon could reply she yawned and turned to walk back to where she was sleeping. When she was halfway across the truck she stopped and turned her head to the side.

"By the way, Mr. Kane, this isn't the first time Gretchen has done something like this. Still I must say you are the first man in a while," said Naomi before walking back to where she was sleeping.

She sat down, leaning her back against the wall of the truck and began to drift off into sleep. Simon had no response except to just whistle to himself. He turned to look back out the moonlit sandy sea beyond. However, unknown to Simon, Mai had been awake for some time and had been listening to the conversation. She brushed the tears that were beginning to form in her eyes aside and tried to forget what she heard before falling asleep.

Chapter 16
The Mad Max Fan Club

They had been driving all through the night and were halfway through the Libyan Desert. Scott wiped the sleep from his face as he pulled over. "What is it?" asked Gretchen, annoyed that they had stopped.

"It's Naomi's turn," said Scott lethargically.

Gretchen sighed. "Fine, I need to stretch my legs anyway," she said as they got out of the truck.

As he walked to the back of the truck, he reached down to the water canteen clipped to his belt and removed it. Eagerly he unscrewed the cap and drank deep of the nourishing water in the canteen. He gasped feeling refreshed as he returned the canteen to his belt. "Naomi, it's your turn to drive!" barked Scott, as he slammed the side of the truck.

Gretchen was standing in the middle of the barren road stretching. Mai was about to get out and say something to Gretchen about Simon. "Hey look over there!" Scott yelled pointing behind them.

Instantly, they all looked and saw two gun trucks rapidly approaching from behind them.

"Oh fuck!" said Gretchen bluntly.

"My sentiments exactly," replied Simon.

"Naomi, Gretchen, get in the truck now! We are leaving!" yelled Scott as he climbed into the back of the truck and manned one of the Browning's along with Simon.

"Not again" muttered Mai as she crouched down nervously.

Naomi got inside the truck and sat behind the wheel and started the engine as Gretchen jumped inside the truck and sat next to Naomi.

"Punch it!" yelled Gretchen.

"You got it," Naomi, replied as she slammed her foot down on the gas pedal.

The truck roared to life and began to move further down the road at ever increasing speeds. Behind them, their pursuers continued to get closer and closer until they were within firing range. "Light em up!" commanded Scott.

Simon and Scott swung their Browning's around and started firing short bursts of hot lead at their pursuers. Inevitably, the gunman on the other trucks began to return fire. Simon and Scott ducked behind the protective walls of the truck. The lead truck slammed into the back of them knocking Simon and Scott back. "Did he seriously just rear end us?" said Gretchen outraged.

"I'm afraid so," replied Naomi dryly.

"Those…. Bastards!" barked Gretchen. "Would you two shoot those assholes, they're ruining my truck!" she yelled as she turned around to face Simon and Scott.

"I didn't know she cared," said Simon sardonically as he and Scott stood up. The other truck drove up beside them on their left; the gunner swung his machine gun around and aimed it at Simons head. Instinctively, Simon pulled out his Jericho and fired two bullets at the gunner's head, killing him instantly. Upon hearing the gunshots Naomi quickly jerked the wheel to the left. As a result, the truck rolled to the left and collided with the enemy truck knocking it to the side. In the cab the driver tried to regain control of his vehicle causing it to swerve from left to right chaotically.

As the truck swerved wildly, Naomi placed her free hand on the butt of her Sig P226R pistol, while her other one kept the wheel straight. Gretchen could tell what she was going to do, she closed her eyes, covered her ears and leaned back in her seat. Naomi slowed down just a little bit until she was at eye level with the driver. In one singular motion, she pulled out her pistol and held out her arm to her left mere inches from Gretchen's face and fired three bullets at the driver's head. Immediately after firing she slammed her foot on the gas and the truck accelerated forward.

Simultaneously, the driver's lifeless body slumped over the wheel. Lacking a driver, the truck careened off the road before flipping onto its side and rolling several feet before crashing into a sand dune and exploding. Naomi blew the smoke off her pistol and returned it to her holster.

"Hell of a shot" muttered Simon as the truck smoldered in ruin behind him.

"That's my Naomi for you," said Scott proudly.

Instinctively, the other truck slowed down while its gunner resumed firing at them. Simon and Scott ducked again waiting for the barrage to end.

"This one's yours Scott" said Simon turning to look at Scott.

"With pleasure Yank" Scott replied dryly. When the truck ceased firing Scott yanked a smoke bomb off of his belt and jumped up. He removed the pin and tossed it through the front window of the truck. Within seconds the bomb detonated filling the cabin with thick black smoke. Scott took advantage of the driver's confusion, manned one of the Browning's and began firing at the engine. Inevitably, the truck exploded before swerving off the road and crashing into a dune.

"Well played," said Simon impressed.

Gretchen stuck her head out the window and raised her fist up high. "Cobalt Express bitches!" she exclaimed Gretchen. Naomi and Scott smiled proudly.

****

Located on the top floor of the Tri-Mark Securities building in Aswan, unknown to everyone in Egypt, resided one of Golem's secret safe houses. This particular safe house was codenamed WATERTOWER. It was manned by a small staff of around five Golem agents, with orders to aid any field agents that needed it. It had a small kitchen, armory, offices and rooms. For the last several days Abner Cohen had been staying there awaiting word on the status of Cobalt's convoy.

At the moment he was standing in the kitchen pouring a cup of coffee. Suddenly, one of the staff, a young man named Adi, burst into the room. "Sir you need to see this?" he said excitedly.

Calmly Abner took a long sip of coffee, "Ok," said Abner having quenched his thirst.

Abner followed him down the hall to the central communications room. The room was where most of the staff spent their days. It was the largest room in the WATERTOWER site. There were desks with computers, each manned by a member of the staff. Adi pointed to one of the staff in the room as they entered.

"Play it," barked Adi.

One of the techs pushed several buttons and a satellite video appeared on the screen. "What is this?" asked Abner, as he took another sip of coffee.

"This is a recording of the latest attack on the convoy, it happened just a few minutes ago," said Adi.

"I see. Any idea who these people are yet?" inquired Abner.

"Not yet Sir, but we're still looking into it" Adi replied.

"Well when you find out let me know," replied Abner as he turned to leave.

"Sir where are you going?" asked Adi.

"To tell the Boss, unless you want to," Abner answered.

"No sir," replied Adi quickly.

"By the way they should be here tomorrow, so go down to the rendezvous point and prep it," said Abner, before leaving the room.

Chapter 17
Hitting the Fan

On days like this when Deng was feeling considerably annoyed by the irritations of his profession, he would go to the shooting range. Located on one of the sublevels beneath the Triads Sankan office, the shooting range featured a state-of-the-art firearms training facility. Upon entering the room, he was surprised to find he wasn't the only one there. Standing at the range, was Dennis Faraday attempting to aim his pistol, a SIG Sauer P230. He was an average looking man with glasses in a white dress shirt and grey pants. The only thing that prevented him from looking like the cubicle worker he once was, was the shoulder holster he had for his pistol.

Standing next to him was Mack Roycewicz, a tall man with the muscular frame of a soldier dressed in brown khakis, and a red and green Hawaiian shirt. Leaning against the back of the room was Siobhan Costello. She was easily the tallest and most dangerous of them despite her appearance. She was a former assassin for the IRA turned Catholic nun and self-proclaimed angel of vengeance. She wore the black and white habit of a Catholic nun with a gold necklace of the cross around her neck.

Deng had spent the past two and a half months tracking these people down so they could assist Simon in finding the Networc. As he entered the room, their attention shifted to him.

"Sup Deng?" asked Mack.

"I thought I'd come down and do some target practice," Deng answered.

"Huh, well I'm trying to show Deadshot here how to shoot," explained Mack as he gestured to Dennis with his thumb.

"Hey man, it's harder than it looks," complained Dennis.

"What about Kane?" Siobhan asked.

"There's been a…complication," answered Deng, deciding to leave out Simon's kidnapping.

"That doesn't sound like the good kind of complication" said Mack.

"There's a good kind of complication?" Dennis asked.

Before any of them could respond Mazin burst into the room out of breath and frantic.

"Dude…breathe" said Mack.

"What is it?" Deng asked.

"Sir, there's a situation in Egypt, we think it might be related to Kane" said Mazin as he gasped for air.

"And that just sounds worse," Dennis observed.

"Come with me," said Deng gesturing to the three of them with his finger. They followed Mazin to the operations room on the floor above them. The operations room resembled the mission control room at NASA. Chinese technicians were sitting at computer consoles working. Facing them was a large monitor on the wall with a map of the world.

"Dude," said Mack stunned at the enormity of the room.

"Impressive, isn't it?" said Deng proudly, as they entered the room.

"Looks like mission control," said Dennis, once again he was reminded how far he had come from his dead-end job in New York.

"Show us" said Deng shifting his attention to Mazin. He nodded and barked some orders to the nearest technician in Mandarin. Instantly breaking news footage from CNN appeared on the screen. The center of the screen was helicopter footage of the Aswan Dam. The words at the bottom of the screen read: Breaking News Terrorist Seize Aswan Dam.

"Not to sound like an ass but..." began Mack.

"When has that stopped you before," interrupted Siobhan.

"Hey!" barked Mack.

"Dude she got you," Dennis laughed.

"Anyway, the attack began several hours ago by now, they've taken the control room and killed all the guards," explained Mazin.

"What does this have to do with Kane and by extension us?" asked Mack.

"What about this complication you mentioned, Deng?" asked Siobhan.

Deng sighed. "Kane and Mai were kidnapped by Cobalt Industries a few days ago," said Deng. "And for the past few days they've been driving across the desert with them."

"And guess who just arrived at Aswan this morning," answered Mazin, as he motioned to the tech. The technician pushed a few buttons and a satellite image of Cobalt's truck appeared on the big screen parked outside a warehouse in Aswan.

"Should we send them in to find out?" asked Mazin pointing to Mack Dennis and Siobhan.

"No, it would take too long to get there" answered Deng. "Besides, Simon's smart, he will get out of this"

"So, what are we supposed to do then? Just sit and watch?" Dennis asked.

"For now, yes, unless you have a better idea?" said Deng.

He shifted his attention back to Mazin. "Hack into the security cameras at the Dam. If you see Simon notify me immediately."

"I have a feeling that these terrorists and Simon are connected," said Deng.

"Yes sir" said Mazin with a nod of his head. Mazin turned and instructed the technician to begin hacking into the security cameras.

"Can they really do this?" whispered Dennis to Mack.

"You see anyone jumping up to stop them?" he replied.

*****

Mai, Simon, Gretchen, Naomi and Scott waited inside the warehouse for what felt like hours. Inside were several wooden crates with various logos on them. Scott and Naomi were working on the truck while Gretchen sat on one of the boxes talking on her phone. Simon was checking his weapons while Mai, still wearing Simon's trench coat, sat on one of the crates staring at Gretchen angrily. Occasionally, Mai would shift her gaze from her to Simon then back to Gretchen. If Gretchen noticed she didn't care as she continued talking on her phone.

Simon put down his rifle and walked over to Mai, positive something was wrong and even more positive that it was his fault. "What's wrong Mai?"

She looked up at him and slid off the crate, her eyes burning with anger. "Like you don't know," she grunted.

"If I knew, I wouldn't be asking," said Simon quietly.

Mai took off the trench coat and tossed it at Simon. "I'm not cold anymore."

Instinctively Simon put the trench coat back on. Before he could think of something else to say, the warehouse door blew off the hinges with a loud bang. While the smoke was still clearing, seven soldiers clad in black body armor helmets and gasmasks each carrying Galil assault rifles, quickly filed into the warehouse. Simon knew exactly who they were, based on their lack of markings, weapons and formation. The soldiers quickly surrounded them aiming their rifles at them.

Instinctively Scott and Naomi drew their weapons.

"Don't" said Simon as he held out his hand.

They lowered their guns cautiously, "do you know these guys Simon?" Gretchen asked.

"Probably" said Simon.

"Not probably, definitely" said a familiar voice. From behind the soldiers a man stepped forward.

In his left hand, handcuffed to his wrist, was a briefcase. He raised his hand and made a fist. In response the soldiers lowered their guns. As he came into view, Simon recognized him immediately as someone he had worked with on various Silhouette missions, the Golem agent codenamed HOPLITE also known as Abner Cohen. He looked at the truck casually and then at Simon with a smug grin of recognition.

"Long time, no see, MONOLITH" said Cohen, with a smug grin.

Chapter 18
Brick In The Wall

"How nice to see you again Mr. HOPLITE" said Gretchen looking up from her phone. She slid off the wooden crate and walked over to him amicably. "Simon, this is..."

"We've met before" Simon interrupted.

"Wunderbar. I love reunions," said Gretchen giddily. "Now then Mr. HOPLITE, let's get down to business."

"With pleasure, you'll get your money after I have spoken to Mr. Kane," replied Abner.

"Well, go and speak to him, he's right here," said Gretchen bluntly as she gestured to him.

"In private," continued Abner correctively.

He looked over at Simon. "Well Simon, shall we?" said Abner as he gestured to the empty office on the other side of the warehouse.

"Whatever you say," grunted Simon as he followed Abner into the office. As the door behind them closed the soldiers positioned themselves in front of the door.

The office consisted of a wooden desk and two chairs that had seen better days. Abner removed the briefcase from his wrist and placed it on the desk. Simon leaned against the wall and crossed his arms. "Been awhile since Beirut, Abner," said Simon.

"I'm glad you remembered," said Abner sarcastically as he typed in the combination to open the briefcase.

"Yeah, I'm known for my memory, but I don't recall Golem making a habit of working with arms dealers," he replied.

"Then your memory isn't as good as you think," said Abner as the briefcase clicked open.

"Now would you mind telling me why you had them drag me across Africa, because I doubt it's about some bombing," asked Simon.

"It's much worse than a mere bombing," said Abner.

Simon raised his eyebrow out of curiosity. "How?"

"Recently we received intel that a rogue faction of the Egyptian army known as the UEF was planning to seize the Aswan Dam and destroy it unless their demands were met," said Abner. "Suffice it to say, that we can't involve ourselves in this matter directly for certain political reasons,"

"So, you hired Gretchen and her stooges to kidnap me and bring me here so I could stop a terrorist attack that you can't stop because of "reasons"?" said Simon.

"Basically," said Abner.

"And the Egyptians can't stop it because...," asked Simon.

"Because it's already happened. Last night the terrorists seized the Dam," answered Abner. "The military are on site but the terrorists have threatened to kill the hostages if they move in."

"Why does Golem care so much about this?" asked Simon.

"Because if the Dam is destroyed it would create chaos in the region that Tel Aviv believes would eventually find its way to Israel," Abner explained.

"Makes sense, but what makes you think they have a bomb powerful enough to destroy the Dam?" asked Simon.

"This" said Abner as he removed a folder from his desk and gave it to Simon. He opened the folder and began reading. His eyes stopped at the words GBU-43/B or as it was more commonly known: the Mother Of All Bombs or MOAB for short.

"Well that changes things" said Simon as he tossed the folder on the desk.

"Now do you see?" asked Abner. "If they detonate that bomb and breach the Dam the resultant flood would kill millions and I know you don't want that on your conscience."

"All right, you can save the sales pitch Abner, I'm in" said Simon. "But there's a problem."

"Go on," said Abner.

"While I'm flattered that you guys think I can take out these assholes and disarm the bomb myself. In reality I'm going to need a team," said Simon.

"Unfortunately, you're going to have to go in yourself because we can't risk one of our men getting identified," Abner countered.

"I never said anything about using your people," said Simon as he glanced outside to Gretchen and the others.

"Wait a minute, you're not serious" he said, instantly aware of what he was implying.

"All I need are Naomi and Scott as support and backup," said Simon.

Abner shook his head. "Absolutely not, it's a miracle they even got you here in the first place," protested Abner.

"True, but do you really want to put the lives of millions of people on the shoulders of one man?" asked Simon.

"Alright fine damnit" said Abner, already regretting having to explain this to Yossi.

"Right then, so do you want to ask them or do you want me to?" asked Simon.

"Might as well be you," said Abner with a shrug as he stood up. The two men walked out of the office and over to Gretchen and the others.

"Well?" Gretchen asked as they walked out of the office.

"Gretchen, we've got an offer for you," said Simon.

She grinned at the words. "Is it an offer I can't refuse?" asked Gretchen sarcastically.

"Too good to decline without due consideration," said Simon slyly.

He spent the next twenty minutes or so telling them about the Dam, being careful to omit any mention of Golem and being careful to only refer to Abner by his codename. They all listened carefully enrapt with what they were hearing. When Simon was finished explaining, they stood silent pensively thinking about his words.

"Dude," said Gretchen finally breaking the silence.

Gretchen looked back at Naomi and Scott, the look on their faces serving as their answer.

"We're in," answered Gretchen.

"There's just one thing," said Gretchen as she shifted her gaze to Abner.

"And that is?" said Abner.

"Double what you paid us to bring Simon here" said Gretchen, her quirkiness suddenly supplanted by a serious tone in her voice.

Abner sighed while Simon couldn't help but grin in amusement. "Fine, and they say my people are obsessed with money," muttered Abner.

As Gretchen and Abner started negotiating Simon noticed that Mai had been listening to the whole thing. He walked over to her not knowing what he was going to say. Mai had a sour disapproving look on her face.

"Mai" began Simon carefully. "What's wrong?"

"You and her," said Mai bluntly, pointing to Gretchen.

"What?" Simon asked.

"You know what I mean. Last night I heard you talking to Naomi about sleeping with Gretchen the other night" said Mai.

"Oh," was all Simon could think to say. Before he could speak Gretchen yelled out his name.

Wearily he turned around to face Gretchen. "Simon, we have an agreement and a plan," said Gretchen motioning to him to come over.

"We'll talk later," said Simon. He turned to join Gretchen and the others.

"See you when I get back" said Simon looking back at Mai. He turned his head and continued walking to Gretchen and the others.

Chapter 19
The House Of Stone

The Aswan Dam stretched across the Nile River. The Dam itself was a massive white structure with ridges on its front. On top of the iconic structure stood rows of power lines and generators. Next to the generators was a windowed structure where the hostages and terrorists were hiding. In front of the Dam was a roadway littered with massive rectangular shipping containers. Located on the far right of the roadway was Simon's point of entry into the labyrinthine innards of the Dam: a large square shaped opening that was large enough for vehicles to pass through.

Simon was dressed in black clothes with a brown holster and belt, all of which had been provided to him by Abner. He was given a small inflatable boat known as a zodiac. He piloted the craft up to the front of the Dam. Simon was glad that the reporters and police were far enough away that they wouldn't be able to see him. Methodically, he scanned the front of the Dam for any movement. Luckily, there was none, he tried not to think about his conversation with Mai. Scott and Naomi were positioned surreptitiously on the sides of the Dam with sniper rifles. Gretchen, Abner and Mai sat miles away watching everything at a hastily constructed headquarters via satellite linkup.

Once Simon was close enough, he placed his hand on his earpiece, "MONOLITH beginning insertion."

"Roger that," replied Abner over the radio.

Simon casually slung the silenced Galil over his shoulder. He then pulled out a small grappling gun about the size of a large pistol. It was a similar model to what he had used while working for Silhouette. He aimed it at the top of the ledge of the roadway and fired.

The grapple barely made any noise as it ejected from the gun and embedded itself in the structure above. Simon tugged on the rope to make sure the grapple was stuck in securely.

He clipped the gun onto his belt and pressed the retrieval button on the back of it. With a barely audible mechanical whine Simon was hoisted into the air up to the roadway. Within minutes he was dangling precariously, mere inches from the ledge. Carefully and quietly, he climbed over the ledge then he removed the grapple from the concrete. He sighed relieved to be on solid ground. Before he could do anything, he heard an angry Arabic voice behind him.

He turned around and saw one of the terrorists aiming an AK-47 at him. Before Simon could respond blood exploded from the man's left eye and he fell on his back, dead. Simon turned around looking behind him. Somewhere on the rocky walls on the left or right of the Nile was Scott and Naomi behind a silenced sniper rifle. He raised his hand and made a thumbs up symbol with his fist as gratitude for saving him. He was sure that they were grinning at the gesture.

Simon switched his attention to his rifle, he slung it off his shoulder and cocked it. With his weapon drawn, he began walking gingerly towards the gaping maw of the square shaped entrance to the facility.

*****

Watching everything from safety was Gretchen, Mai and Abner. They were watching everything on a computer via satellite and news coverage on television. "Well, he's making his way inside" said Abner relieved that everything had gone according to plan so far.

Mai watched the screens feeling out of her element while Gretchen and Abner looked at the screens looking as disaffected as possible. Gretchen was drinking a cup of coffee as they watched the screen.

"I must say Miss Neubauer, your people are quite impressive, that shot alone was incredible," said Abner.

"Yes, if someone's going to be watching my ass, I prefer they be good at their job," said Gretchen smugly as she raised the coffee cup to her lips.

"My God, what is wrong with you people?" asked Mai in frustration. "You just watched someone get killed and all you can think of is how well it was done?"

"Well, not all we can think of" said Gretchen meekly.

"Oh yeah then what else?" Mai asked.

"Well for starters this coffee is terrible," said Gretchen dryly as she held up the coffee cup.

At a loss for words and fed up with what she was seeing Mai stormed out of the building. As she stood outside, she thought about Simon. A few minutes later Abner joined her outside. "What do you want?" she asked.

"Only to help" said Abner calmly.

"And how do you intend to do that?" Mai asked.

"By offering an explanation" said Abner. "There are people that take no pleasure in the demands of this life, and there are people that are consumed by this life" continued Abner.

Mai shrugged knowing that Gretchen had clearly been consumed by it. "So what side are you and Simon on?"

"I'd like to think I'm the former, but Simon he's neither he survives this life," answered Abner. "By the way I know it's none of my business, but I overheard your conversation with him"

Mai looked at him surprised, "It's obvious that you two mean more to each other than you want the other to know," said Abner.

"Your point?" she asked.

"Regardless of what he did he still said goodbye to you" said Abner.

Abner could tell that his words had struck a chord in her. "Come inside, it's not safe out here."

Mai shrugged and followed him inside the warehouse and back to the room with the screens.

Chapter 20
The Dancing Puppets

Counselor Cathcart placed his feet on the desk of the Dam's director and leaned back in the chair. The director's office could have been mistaken for the office of any powerful CEO. Behind the desk was a massive window overlooking the entirety of the Dam. The hostages were on the floor below locked in a room cowering. Counselor Cathcart reached into the desk and pulled out a bottle of scotch and a few glasses.

As he was about to pour a glass of the scotch into the glasses General Faisel burst into the room, a worried look on his face. "Is there a problem General?" asked Counselor

Cathcart dryly as he poured the scotch into the glasses.

"We have an intruder" said Faisel gruffly.

Cathcart looked up at him surprised. "Who is it? Special Forces?"

"No, someone else" replied Faisel.

Cathcart sighed as he drank the scotch and stood up. "You said your men were good, clearly you were wrong"

Faisel grimaced at him, angry at the insult but too afraid to say or do anything.

"Show me" said Cathcart as he stood up. He followed Faisel to the security room located two floors down.

Upon entering the room, the two men were greeted by a wall of TV screens each showing video from one of the many security cameras around the complex. Seated at a desk behind one of the screens was one of Faisel's soldiers. The man stood up and saluted General Faisel when they entered. Counselor Cathcart rolled his eyes as General Faisel dismissed him.

"Show us the video of the intruder," ordered Faisel.

The soldier nodded and sat down behind a computer and began pressing multiple buttons. After a few seconds he pointed to one of the screens, "that's him."

Cathcart and Faisel looked at the screen studiously. It showed a man rappelling to the front roadway. As they continued watching they saw one of Faisels men get shot. Cathcart noticed that there was something about the man that made him look familiar. "Rewind and zoom in on the intruder."

The man pressed a few buttons and the screen rewound, then stopped and zoomed in on a frame of the man's face. Suddenly Counselor Cathcart recognized him from a description. *It was him: Simon Kane* he thought.

Faisel could tell by the look in his eyes that he knew the man. Counselor Cathcart turned to face Faisel. "He's going for the bomb, General tell your men to find him and bring him to me," said Cathcart sternly.

"Who is he?" asked Faisel.

"General, did I tell you to find him or to ask me who he is?" said Counselor Cathcart.

General Faisel pulled out his walkie-talkie and began to speak into it. When he had finished Counselor Cathcart pulled out his pistol and cocked it. He turned to leave the room.

"Where are you going?" asked Faisel.

"To guard the bomb," Cathcart answered.

*****

Simon moved stealthily through the cavernous facility trying not to think about how the terrorists could blow the bomb any minute. The inside of the Dam was a long dimly lit corridor littered with wooden crates and shipping containers. Simon heard voices and instinctively jumped behind one of the shipping containers. He peeked out and saw two UEF guards carrying Ak-47's talking across from a door marked Turbines in Arabic. Simon holstered his rifle, he flicked back his wrist and his wrist blade popped out.

He took a deep breath and ran out from behind the crate. He ran straight at the guard with his back to him and before either guard knew what had happened Simon jammed the blade into the back of the guard's neck. The other guards face was a look of shock and terror. Before he could raise his weapon Simon pulled the blade out and slit his throat with it. The man fell to the floor bleeding next to his compatriot. Simon removed the blood from the knife by wiping it on the uniforms of the two dead men. Calmly he slid it back into the band on his wrist.

Just as Simon put the blade back into the bracelet, a guard opened the door and walked out. The first thing he saw were the two dead bodies of his comrades laying on the floor. Slowly his eyes drifted to Simon, instinctively the guard reached for his pistol. Simon drew his silenced Jericho and shot him first. "Too slow" muttered Simon.

Simon returned the Jericho to its holster and drew his Galil as he gingerly approached the door. He positioned himself next to the door and opened it slowly. He looked inside trying not to squint at the light as he scanned for any enemies. The door opened into a massive room with four humming hydroelectric turbines. Having found no enemies, Simon slowly walked inside. On the other side of the room was a door that led to the supply warehouse.

Simon ran across the room determined not to waste any more time. Suddenly two guards walked into the room and began firing at him. Simon jumped behind one of the turbines. In front of him were two guards taking cover behind a wall. Simon waited till he had a good shot at the guards. One of them peeked their head out from behind the wall to aim. Simon leaned out from cover, aimed and fired at him with the Galil, killing him.

The other guard ran towards the door on the other side while firing his gun. Simon shifted his aim to the other man and fired two rounds at him. With the two guards dispatched Simon ran to the door on the other side of the room. According to the schematics that Abner had given him the bomb would be in the supply warehouse on the other side of the door. Simon kicked open the door and entered the warehouse.

The warehouse consisted of more shipping containers and machinery. On the other side of the room was a ladder that went to a control room overlooking the warehouse. Simon could hear someone barking orders in Arabic on the other side of the shipping containers. Surreptitiously Simon walked around the shipping container, he peeked around and saw General Faisel ordering five of his troops. He was dressed in a khaki military suit with a pistol attached to his brown belt. Simon slung the rifle over his shoulder.

Simon quickly snuck up behind him and before anyone could react wrapped his arm around Faisel's neck. With his other hand Simon pulled his pistol out of the holster and aimed it at the men. "All right the game is up assholes, drop the guns now!" yelled Simon in Arabic.

"You bastard," Faisel growled as he tried to free himself from Simon. "I mean it. Drop the damn guns!"

"Shoot this bastard now!" ordered Faisel.

In the control room Counselor Cathcart was quite amused by what he was seeing below. He briefly thought about intervening but decided against it, wishing to see how it ended.

The guards raised their guns and aimed them at Simon. "Well…shit," he grunted.

Simon fired two bullets at one of the guards then another and another. The remaining two opened fire on Simon. Simon backed away instinctively behind the shipping container as the remaining two gunmen ran for cover. As Faisel struggled to free himself from Simons grip, Simon leaned out and fired at them with Faisel's pistol. Enraged at seeing his men murdered Faisel brought his foot down on Simons foot causing his grip on him to loosen enough to break free. He hit Simon in the face with his left elbow. Faisel quickly reached into his boot and pulled out a hidden knife then he spun around. Simon quickly recovered from the blow to the face and saw the knife coming at him.

"You know what they say about knives and gunfights General?" said Simon as he aimed the pistol at Faisel.

He pulled the trigger but instead of hearing a loud bang and smelling cordite there was nothing but a click. "It helps if you have ammo," said Faisel with a cocky grin.

"Shit" grunted Simon. He tossed the pistol at Faisel hitting him in the head.

Taking advantage of the distraction, Simon snapped his wrist back causing the blade to pop out of his wrist band and lunged towards him. With his other hand he got Faisel in a headlock and then plunged his wrist blade into Faisels stomach repeatedly. He let him go and he fell to the ground quickly bleeding to death.

"Thanks for the advice" said Simon dryly as he pulled out his Jericho. Simon ran to the ladder and climbed up to the control room.

Chapter 21
Face Of The Enemy

The control room consisted of a large window, a computer console and in the middle of the room sat the bomb. Eagerly Simon ran over to it when he felt a sharp pain on the back of his neck that caused him to fall forward.

"Welcome to the party Mr. Kane," said a voice standing behind him. Wearily, Simon looked up at the man. He looked as if he had seen a ghost. The man had the same plain facial features and smug voice as Counselor Black. He was even dressed in the same clothes as Counselor Black when he killed

Sheila. He stood over Simon aiming a gun at his head.

"I killed you," grunted Simon.

The man smiled. "No, you killed Counselor Black, all Counselors look the same, mandatory plastic surgery, I am Counselor Cathcart," said the man proudly with a smug smirk.

"That supposed to mean anything?" asked Simon sarcastically.

His face contorted into an expression of rage upon hearing the question. "It should. You killed my colleague a few months ago in Belarus," said Counselor Cathcart.

"You expecting an apology from me?" Simon growled.

"No. I expect nothing, I demand that you die, " said Cathcart furiously.

"Is that why you sent those goons to kill me and the others in the desert?" said Simon.

"Actually, that was Mr. Zero, your interference in this operation was unexpected," said Counselor Cathcart but I must say it is quite salubrious, that you have shown up since now I can avenge Counselor Black by killing you."

Simon recognized the name as the same name that one of the assassins uttered before his death.

"So why are you working with the UEF to blow up the Dam?" he asked.

"Why do people do anything? For money and power," answered Cathcart. "You see, once the Dam is destroyed, the unrest would allow us to install Faisel as the new President of Egypt."

"And then, you assholes could pull the strings of the Egyptian government," said Simon.

"Indeed, Mr. Kane" answered Cathcart smugly.

"It's too late for Faisel," grunted Simon.

"Yes well…they are going to need to hire someone to help with the rebuilding and that someone will be us" Cathcart replied. "Either way we still win.'"

"As for you Mr. Kane it's time to say goodnight," continued the Counselor as he pulled back the hammer on the pistol.

"Sorry, but I'm not tired," said Simon as he kicked Cathcart's legs out from under him. He jumped to his feet, grabbed Cathcart by his jacket collar and threw him at the console. Before Cathcart could move or do anything Simon was in front of him. Simon punched him across the face, followed by a blow to the stomach with his knee. Simon then grabbed him by his jacket.

"I know what you're thinking, how come he's kicking my ass?" growled Simon. "Well, I knew I'd run into you bastards again, so I've been preparing for this."

"Now where and who is Mr. Zero?" asked Simon.

Cathcart laughed almost hysterically, "you'll never know."

As he finished speaking there was a crack and Cathcarts mouth started to foam and his body began to shake as if he was having a seizure. Simon let him go, knowing exactly what was happening to him.

He had seen it enough times in Silhouette to recognize the symptoms of ingesting it. "Cyanide," muttered Simon as he looked at the grisly corpse in front of him, foam beginning to bubble out of Cathcarts mouth.

He looked away in disgust and walked over to the bomb and he carefully examined it. He breathed a sigh of relief upon seeing that it wasn't on a timer. He kneeled down and took a deep breath, slowly he began carefully disarming the bomb. After several minutes he managed to disconnect the detonator from the payload making the bomb effectively useless. He stood up and put his hand up to his earpiece communicator.

"MONOLITH to HOPLITE, mission accomplished proceeding to LZ now" said Simon.

"Roger that" answered Abner over the communicator.

Simon took one last look at Cathcart's body before climbing back down the ladder and quickly walked back to the boat.

*****

On the other side of the world in Sankan, Deng, Siobhan, Dennis and Mack were sitting in the office in the control room. Mack was eating from a bag of potato chips while Siobhan, Deng and Dennis were watching the technicians outside. Suddenly, Deng's assistant Mazin burst into the office excitedly.

"This is getting repetitive Mazin" said Deng dryly.

"Sir we found him," Mazin replied excitedly. The four of them followed Mazin to the control room without saying a word. On the main screen was a black and white image of Simon running through the halls of the Dam.

"Well done Mazin. Well done indeed" said Deng.

"So that's him?" asked Mack as he reached into the bag for more chips.

"Yes, and incidentally you may have to go get him" said Deng.

"Why? Can't he just come here to Sankan on his own?" Dennis asked.

"Normally yes, but I'm not leaving anything to chance" said Deng.

"Mazin, monitor all flights going out of Egypt, don't lose them" said Deng.

"Yes sir" replied Mazin.

"Shit, I'm out of chips," grunted Mack as he threw the bag into a nearby trash can.

"Seriously?" asked Dennis looking at him half incredulously.

"We may have to go get this guy and you're worried about running out of chips?" continued Dennis.

"Hey man, don't sweat the petty things and don't pet the sweaty things," replied Mack dismissively.

"What does that even mean?" asked Dennis.

"Don't worry about the small stuff," answered Mack.

"How is this small stuff?" asked Dennis.

Mack shrugged. "Could be worse."

"How?" replied Dennis.

"Could be big stuff" answered Mack dryly.

"Agreed," said Deng.

Chapter 22
Damage Control

The Networc's Board of Directors rarely, if ever, held emergency meetings, yet they were having one today.

"Alright, people clearly shit happened, I want to know why," began Mr. Zero.

In their offices across the world the various members of the board squirmed nervously.

"The failure of Project: MOSES is a serious one, but it is not so serious that it presented a serious cost to our interests. Isn't that right Mr. Five?" said Mr. Zero.

"Yes," Mr. Five answered.

"I think the immediate problem is Simon Kane," interjected Mr. Seven.

"Quite right Mr. Seven," Mr. Zero replied.

"Perhaps we should consider hiring someone to kill him," stated Mr. Six.

"My men are perfectly capable of killing one man," said Mr. One angrily.

"Mr. One, this man has thwarted our designs twice. He must not be allowed to do it again," said Mr. Zero scoldingly. "Do you have anyone in mind Mr. Six?"

"Yes actually, we don't hire them too often but I believe posting an open contract on him to the Guild is our best option," answered Mr. Six.

"Interesting idea. Do it Mr. Six," answered Mr. Zero.

"Now then, Mr. Two, update me on the status of Project: GHOST FIRE," said Mr. Zero.

*****

By the time Simon, Naomi and Scott returned to the warehouse the news was already reporting how Egyptian Special Forces had stormed the Dam and saved the hostages. As they pulled up to the front of the compound

Abner, Gretchen and Mai were standing outside waiting for them.

"Welcome back guys!" said Gretchen gleefully as they disembarked from the truck.

"That was quite impressive Simon," Abner said as the two men shook hands.

"Just like in Beirut," said Simon slyly. "What now?"

"Well, Mai told me how you were originally heading to Sankan for some reason so we'll be flying you to Dubai where you can get a connecting flight," answered Abner.

"Thanks," said Simon. "When's the flight?"

"Immediately, I'm afraid we have to get you all out of the country as soon as possible to minimize our involvement in this affair" answered Abner. "However, once you're in Dubai you'll have to find your own way to Sankan."

"I understand, no loose ends, right?" Simon replied. Abner shrugged in response.

"What about them?" he asked pointing to Scott, Naomi and Gretchen.

"Don't worry about us lover boy, we've been paid, and we'll be on the first plane back to Athens," said Gretchen.

"So, I guess that's it then? We just disappear?" asked Mai.

"Pretty much," answered Simon. Just then two black cars drove up to the warehouse.

"They'll take you to separate airports," Abner explained. They all nodded in understanding, Scott and Simon shook hands.

"It's been nice working with you Yank," said Scott.

"Likewise," answered Simon.

Simon and Naomi shook hands next before they walked over to one of the cars. Finally, Gretchen walked up to him and embraced him before kissing him on the cheek.

"Thanks for a hell of a night," Gretchen whispered softly into his ear.

"You never told me the story about that tattoo," replied Simon flirtatiously as she let him go.

Gretchen grinned at his remark. "Perhaps some other time mein sexy cowboy," she said as she walked over to the car. She got inside closed the door and rolled down the window. She leaned out the window as Scott started the engine and blew Simon a kiss as they drove away.

"Bitch," muttered Mai with a disapproving shrug.

"Don't worry Mai, she's nothing compared to you," said Simon with a grin.

Mai couldn't help but blush as she walked to the car.

"Smooth," said Abner.

"Jealous?" replied Simon.

Abner laughed. "She loves you I think,"

"I hope not, women that love me have an awfully short lifespan," said Simon dismissively, before walking over to the car and getting in.

Once he was inside the car he started the engine and drove off into the desert.

"Well?" asked Simon.

"I think we could use a rest before going back to Sankan," said Mai.

"I think you're right. Any ideas?" asked Simon.

"Well, my father has an executive suite at the Burj Khalifa," said Mai with a sly grin.

"Mai, I like the way you think" Simon replied.

*****

On Sankan in the office adjacent to the control room, Deng, Siobhan, Mack and Dennis were waiting anxiously for word on Simon and Mai. Mazin walked in, "I have good news and I have bad news," said Mazin simply.

"Good please," said Deng.

"They just boarded a private plane belonging to Tri-Mark Securities bound for Dubai," answered Mazin.

"And the bad news?" Siobhan asked.

"The Guild just put out an open contract on Simon worth ten million dollars," said Mazin.

Mack raised his eyebrows in surprise. "Damn! That'll bring out every Guild assassin available,"

"Exactly, which is why you three are going to Dubai to get them and bring them back here before some Guild asshole kills them, no offense Mack," said Deng.

"None taken," replied Mack.

"How are we going to find them?" Siobhan asked.

"Well, besides the fact that an American wearing a trench coat and an eye patch traveling with a Chinese woman kind of stick out in a crowd, they'll most likely be going to the Burj," said Deng.

"Swanky," said Mack.

"Any particular reason?" asked Dennis.

"Mai's father has a luxury suite there," Deng answered.

Chapter 23
Money To Burn

Simon looked out the window of their room at the Burj Khalifa. From the one hundred and third floor of the tower the view of the city and surrounding sea of desert was nothing short of breathtaking. The suite had three bedrooms, a fully-stocked kitchen and in the living room a brown leather wrap-around couch that was sunk into the floor facing a wide panoramic window that overlooked the city of Dubai. Mai had informed Simon upon arriving that the master bedroom on the far end was hers and the second smallest room was his.

"Enjoying the view?" she asked.

Simon turned around so he could face her. Mai was dressed in a white bathrobe; her hair and skin still damp from the shower. "Absolutely."

Mai blushed and immediately tried to hide it.

"So how long have you been coming here?" asked Simon.

"My father brought me here once for my birthday," answered Mai.

"Hell of a birthday present, my Dad got me a bike for my birthday," said Simon sarcastically.

Mai couldn't help but laugh. "Do you feel like having dinner with me?"

"You asking me on a date?" asked Simon sarcastically.

"Am I?" replied Mai, with a sly inviting grin. Ever since that night in Tangier it felt like an impermeable wall had been building higher and higher between them. Now it seemed like that wall was suddenly shrinking. If Simon was being honest with himself, he welcomed it but he also knew in his heart of hearts that if the wall continued to shrink Mai would be in more danger, still he couldn't help himself.

"Well if you are my answer is yes," Simon answered coolly.

Mai smiled warmly at the answer. "Then I guess I had better get ready."

"Any idea where we'd be going on this date?" asked Simon.

Mai grinned. "Well there is a restaurant on Level 122 called Atmosphere," answered Mai.

"Sounds out of this world," replied Simon dryly.

Mai smirked at the bad joke. "I'll go make a reservation," she replied before turning to leave for the bedroom.

It was strange the other day in Egypt she was mad at him but now it appeared her mood had softened. He was curious what brought about this change in her mood. "By the way I'll have a suit brought up for you. Atmosphere isn't the kind of place you go to looking like that, also a shower wouldn't hurt either," said Mai smugly before she closed the bedroom door.

Simon smirked and then looked at his reflection in the mirror and smelled himself.

"Damn" he muttered as he realized how bad he looked.

He reeked of sweat and blood, his shirt and pants had rips in them. His appearance was not unexpected as the last time he had a shower was the morning after his night with Gretchen. He shrugged his shoulders and walked to his room. It was smaller than the other two rooms, but it still had the usual amenities of an upper-class hotel room such as its own bathroom and shower off to the side. He walked into the bathroom and removed his clothes.

He turned on the hot water and got in the shower. The water was nice and warm making him feel more relaxed then he had in days. When he had finished with his shower, he dried himself off then put on one of the complimentary bathrobes. He then lay down on the bed and fell asleep.

*****

Simon awoke to the sound of someone knocking on the door of the suite. Lethargically he glanced at the clock on the table next to his bed and was surprised to see that he had been asleep for several hours. He got out of the bed and put on the black complimentary slippers that came with the room. He walked to the door of the room and opened it. Standing in front of him was one of the hotel staff holding a large black bag with a hanger hook sticking out of the top.

"Your suit Sir," said the man with a courteous smile.

"Thank you, that'll be all," Simon replied politely as he accepted the suit. He closed the door as the attendant walked away. Simon walked back to his room and placed the bag on the bed and unzipped it. He was pleasantly surprised to see that it was a black tuxedo made by Tom Ford. He held it up by the coat hanger so he could examine it in more detail; it consisted of a double-breasted black dinner jacket, bow tie and pants with a white silk shirt and black dress shoes. He wondered how Mai knew what his sizes were but decided against asking.

Suddenly there was a knock on the door, Simon turned to answer it and opened the door. He was greeted by Mai who was still in her bathrobe. Mai had a surprised look on her face as she had never seen Simon in anything other than his regular clothes. Quickly she regained her composure and adjusted her glasses. "I heard the knock on the door, did your tux arrive?"

"Yeah, it's quite a monkey suit," replied Simon.

"I'm glad you like it, by the way our dinner reservation is in a half hour," said Mai.

"Thanks, I'll get ready" Simon said. The two nodded at each other and Mai returned to her room to get ready. Simon closed the door and walked to the bedroom to look in the mirror. He noticed a jar of hair gel next to the faucet and used it to smooth his hair back giving it a sleek distinguished look. Then he returned to the bedroom, removed the bathrobe and put on the tuxedo. Before he put on the dinner jacket he glanced at his gun and holster resting on the bed stand.

Simon decided to put on the holster in case something happened especially since he felt naked without it. He put the dinner jacket on next, so it covered his gun. He put on his watch and walked into the living room to wait for Mai. The sun had begun to set drenching the room in a cool orange glow.

"Ready to go," said Mai as she walked out of her room.

Simon turned to face her and was amazed at how different she looked. She was wearing a tight long, short-sleeved, black cheongsam dress with red stripes around the edges and collar and black high-heels. The tight dress accentuated the natural curves in her body that had previously been hidden. Her long black hair was tied up in a bun. Simon found it hard to believe he was looking at the same woman that a few days ago resembled a bookish nerd. Mai adjusted her glasses and grinned. "Like what you see?" Mai asked.

"You certainly look different," answered Simon.

"Thanks, you clean up pretty well yourself, now shall we go?" asked Mai.

"After you," replied Simon gesturing to the door with his hand. She walked out of the room and he followed her to the elevator.

Chapter 24
The Glittering Kingdom

They entered the Atmosphere Restaurant and were immediately shown to a table by the maître d. The restaurant was an opulent dimly lit room with a bar against the wall facing windows that stretched from the floor to the ceiling. Simon ignored the bar and the liquor as best as he could. As they followed the waiter to their table the other patrons glared at them asking each other in whispers who they were and why the man in the tuxedo had an eye patch. Simon and Mai barely noticed or acknowledged them as they followed the man to their table and sat down. Their table was up against the window overlooking the oasis of money and power that is Dubai.

Upon sitting down, they glanced out the window at the city. The starry skies above and the twinkling city below were almost indistinguishable from each other as they sparkled in the darkness like diamonds. "I must say Mai, you certainly picked a hell of a restaurant," said Simon as he looked back at her.

"Wait till you try the food. It's to die for," she answered.

"I'll bet it is," Simon replied.

"You know it's funny, a few days ago we were riding in a gun truck across the Sahara now we're here in Dubai dressed to kill," said Mai with a grin.

Simon grinned in response, "Yeah, it's always interesting seeing what tomorrow brings," said Simon.

One of the waiters walked over to the table carrying menus and water. The waiter asked what they wanted to drink. "Tea, sweetened with no lemon," ordered Simon.

"Reisling" she ordered.

The waiter nodded and walked away. They read their menus quietly, each deciding what to have. Simon decided to have the prime rib, while Mai chose to have the filet mignon. A few minutes later the waiter returned carrying their drinks. They told him what they wanted to have once again he nodded and walked away with the menus.

"I'm surprised, I didn't expect you to order tea," said Mai, as Simon took a sip of his tea.

"Well what did you expect?" asked Simon.

"Beer, wine, vodka something alcoholic" answered Mai.

"Actually, I don't drink, me and the bottle had an…. unhealthy relationship," Simon answered.

"Interesting, it seems I've met the only superspy that doesn't drink," replied Mai.

"Well, I wouldn't say super, but I appreciate the compliment, we can't all be James Bond" said Simon smugly as he drank from his glass.

"I'm sure," she replied with an amused grin.

They were so engrossed in their conversation that they didn't notice two waiters approaching their table carrying their food. "It smells excellent," said Mai as the waiters placed their dishes in front of them. The waiters smiled and nodded before disappearing back into the kitchen.

"I've been thinking about you and Gretchen," said Mai softly.

Simon sighed as he placed his utensils on the table. As she said the words he saw the beginning of tears in her eyes. Instantly, she brushed them away as if they were nothing.

"I've been thinking about it. I don't blame you for it but all I want to know is did it mean anything, do you love her?" asked Mai as she brushed away more tears from her eyes in an effort to hide them.

"Mai, that night with Gretchen meant nothing to her or me it was just a one-night stand for both of us," said Simon solemnly.

"You sure?" asked Mai.

"Absolutely," he replied.

Mai smiled looking almost relieved at his answer. "Then that's all I need to hear,"

"I'm glad. So, what now?" asked Simon.

"I know a place with a great view," asked Mai with a smile.

"Show me," said Simon, they stood up, paid for their meal and walked out of the club to the nearest elevator. The elevator rose higher and higher until it stopped on floor 125, marked observatory. They walked out of the elevator into a large vacant room illuminated by soft blue light and the distant stars. On the other end of the room were couches facing panoramic windows. Soft music rained down on them from speakers above.

"It's beautiful isn't it," asked Mai as they looked out at the city lights which seemed as distant and ethereal as the stars above.

"Yes, it is," said Simon, looking at Mai.

"Though I wasn't talking about the view," said Simon with a smile. Mai smiled and held his hand, before they knew it they were holding each other in their arms. They began swaying back and forth to the soft music playing above.

"I hope this never ends Simon," whispered Mai.

"Don't worry Mai, we'll always have this now and forever," said Simon softly.

They continued swaying back and forth holding each in their arms. It was as if the world beyond had ceased to exist and all that is and ever would be was this moment.

Chapter 25
Million Dollar Rundown

The next day Simon and Mai chose not to talk about their recent adventure. They occupied their time by enjoying the copious amenities of the Burj Khalifa, and each other's company. She told Simon that there was a lovely outdoor café in the market not far from the Burj Khalifa. Lacking anything else to do they decided to go to the café that afternoon. The marketplace was inundated with all sorts of humanity. It was a beautiful afternoon with the hot desert sun raining down on the coastal city.

Simon kept close to Mai in case someone tried anything malevolent. He was dressed in his long gray pants, black t-shirt and dark blue trench coat while Mai was wearing blue jeans and a white collared shirt and glasses. The cafe was a in a small courtyard surrounded by worn stone pillars. Simon and Mai sat at one of metal tables in the shade. Simon ordered coffee while Mai ordered an iced tea.

"How's the coffee?" began Mai after taking a sip.

Simon didn't hear her; he was too busy scanning the area. They were the only two diners at the café, though he did notice two pale identical looking men with long brown hair dressed in a black dress shirt and pants. One of them wore a red tie the other a purple one, each carrying a violin case. They walked across the courtyard to the cafe.

Upon getting the bounty on Simon Kane, Razlov Konov and his identical twin brother Dazlov set out to find them. They were fairly easy to track as Simons eye patch made him stand out. They tracked them through the market to the café. Upon seeing them at the table drinking coffee they smiled like a hunter that had finally located prey.

Their weapons concealed inside the violin cases. They hid behind the pillars as they slowly removed two silenced G36c rifles from the violin cases. "Shall we shoot the Chinese woman as well Mr. Dazzle?" Razlov asked childishly.

"I don't see why not Mr. Razzle," replied Dazlov as the two men cocked and loaded their rifles.

They leaned behind the pillars, "I'll take Mr. Kane," said Razlov. "Very well Mr. Razlov, I'll take the woman," replied Dazlov. They kissed each other on the lips before aiming their rifles at the heads of Simon and Mai.

Simon saw a glint of metal coming from the pillars with his one good eye. He looked at it and recognized to his horror the cylindrical barrel of a suppressor. "Mai, get down now!" yelled Simon as he flipped the metal table on its side. She recognized the tone in his voice and got behind the table. He joined her behind the table just as a soundless barrage of bullets began to hit the table.

"Gotta say Mai I'm not a fan of the service here," said Simon as he drew his pistol and instinctively cocked it. He waited for an opportunity to return fire at their unseen attackers, both of them hoping the table would protect them for a little longer.

"Mai, keep your head down!" yelled Simon.

"Who are these people?" Mai replied anxiously.

"That's a good question," Simon muttered.

Suddenly the fusillade of steel and lead ended. "Perfect," he muttered. Simon jumped up and fired three shots at the attackers who jumped behind the pillars.

"I don't think he wants to die Mr. Razzle," said Dazlov sarcastically.

"I don't think so either, Mr. Dazzle," Razlov replied as the two men reloaded their weapons. With their weapons reloaded they began returning fire, Simon immediately ducked back behind the table. The brothers were about to step out of the shadows and start moving closer to them when suddenly three shots from the side rang out forcing them back behind the pillars. Simon and Mai looked over at the direction of the shots. They were surprised to see a tall blonde white man in black tea shade sunglasses in a red and green Hawaiian shirt with and khakis aiming an FN SCAR assault rifle at their hidden attackers.

"Yo eye patch! Cavalries here!" said the man in a boisterous New Jersey accent.

"Friend of yours?" asked Mai.

"Hopefully," Simon grunted.

"Simon! Mai! We'll lay down covering fire, get your asses over here now!" yelled the man. Before Simon could reply, a tall curvaceous woman with red hair, dressed like a nun, carrying an M60 walked out from behind the man and began firing at the twins.

The man's identity was alien to Simon however Deng had introduced Simon to the woman before, he tried to remember her name. "I didn't know the damn circus was in town,"

"What do we do?" asked Mai.

Simon considered the options carefully. "Run over to those two on three."

"What about you?" asked Mai.

"I'll be right behind you" said Simon with a cocky grin that reassured Mai.

"All right one, two three!" yelled Simon.

Mai ran as fast as she could to the man in the Hawaiian shirt. Simon stood up and followed behind her firing bullets at the twins. They followed the man and the woman out of the café through the market to a black SUV at the entrance of the bazaar. Simon and Mai jumped into the back seat while the man and the woman jumped into the seat in front of them. "Dennis, drive now!" yelled the man, Simon and the woman slammed the doors shut.

The man he called Dennis was an average looking man in a white dress shirt black tie, and gray pants with glasses. The car sped up and pulled away from the bazaar. The blonde man turned around and faced Simon and Mai.

"By the way I'm Mack and that's Siobhan" said the blonde man as he gestured to the nun. Before Simon or Mai could express their gratitude, Mack aimed a peculiar looking gun at Simon and fired a small dart at his chest.

"And this is a dart gun" said Mack as he swung around, aimed the pistol at Mai and shot her with the gun. Upon being hit with the dart they both fell over unconscious.

Mack then turned back to face Dennis. "Dennis, the airport and step on it."

Chapter 26
Return to the Black Kingdom

Simon awoke to a loud knocking sound; he rubbed his head exhaustedly. He looked around and saw that he was in a hotel room, lying on a bed still in his regular clothes.

"Great, this shit again," muttered Simon. He got off the bed and walked to the door where the banging was coming from. Simon opened the door and saw Mai standing in the doorway.

"So, we're back on Sankan," said Mai.

"Yep," replied Simon.

"Deng wants to see us in his office," said Mai.

Simon shrugged. "Let's go."

He followed Mai to the elevator at the end of the hallway. Mai and Simon rode the elevator to the top floor. They walked down a long hallway, at the end of it were two wooden doors that opened the door into a large ornate office. There were bookcases on the left and right walls; the back wall was a giant panoramic window. In the center of the room was a large wooden desk. In front of the desk were two chairs.

Seated behind the desk in a black and white suit was Deng. Standing on his right was Siobhan, standing on his left was Mack and the driver named Dennis. "Welcome to the party Mr. Kane, please take a seat," said Deng.

"You know, if you want to have a word with me you can just ask, there's no need to dart gun me every single time," said Simon as they sat down.

"I'll keep that in mind," Deng replied sarcastically.

"Anyway, do you remember six months ago when we made our deal?" said Deng. "Well allow me to introduce the team I promised to assemble for you."

"Let's see you already introduced me to Siobhan, the guy in the Hawaiian shirt is Mack and the nerdy looking guy in glasses is Dennis. Is that right?" asked Simon.

"How did you know my name?" Dennis asked.

"Mack told you to drive back in Dubai" he answered.

"He called you nerdy looking," said Mack mockingly.

"So, you spend six months assembling a team and you show up with a nerd, a nun and blonde Magnum PI" groused Simon.

"I promise Simon there's more to these people than meets the eye," Deng protested.

"I hope so" Simon muttered.

"Who were those guys trying to kill us back in Dubai?" asked Mai.

"Assassins, it seems the Networc is tired of having their grand designs foiled by you Simon. So, they've decided to put a hit out on you," answered Deng.

"Those two in particular are known as the Razzle Dazzle Twins, members of the assassin's Guild" Mack replied.

Simon sighed. "So where do we go from here?"

Deng smiled slyly. "Mai, since it is too dangerous for you to be around Simon the Mountain Master has ordered you to be transferred to his retreat in the Japanese Alps."

Mai was shocked. "Those are his orders, I'm sorry," said Deng.

"That's clever" said Simon before Mai could issue a word of protest. Mai thought about it for a minute and realized he was right. This was the best course of action, she just didn't want to be separated from him.

"So, what about me?" Simon queried.

"You will be here with the team to take down the Networc while we work to find intelligence on them" answered Deng.

"Sounds like you have it all figured out," replied Simon, impressed with Deng's forethought.

"We never do anything halfway," he replied.

"How long will it take you to find intel on them?" asked Simon.

"It depends. Hopefully in a few weeks since all our operatives across the globe have been instructed to make obtaining intel on the Networc top priority" Deng answered. Simon wasn't surprised at his answer.

Suddenly he remembered the name Cathcart mentioned at the Dam. "Tell your people to look for the name Mr. Zero it has some connection with the Networc."

"How do you know that name?" asked Deng.

"Long story short we had a run-in with a Networc assassin in Africa who said the name before he died," answered Simon.

"Will do, anything else?" asked Deng.

"No" answered Simon.

"What about those assassins that came after us?" asked Mai.

"Good question, Simon is the only one the Guild put a target on. Your father wants you sent to a safe house regardless," answered Deng.

Deng sensed the conversation was over, so he stood up. "Now then Mai, a helicopter is waiting on the roof to take you to the airport where a plane is waiting to fly you to Japan," he said gesturing to the door.

Simon, Mai, Mack, Siobhan and Dennis followed Deng out of his office to the elevator. They rode it up to the top floor where they walked up to the roof via a short flight of stairs. Upon reaching the roof they were greeted by four Chinese men in black suits and black sunglasses holding submachine guns standing around a small helicopter. "Well Mai, I guess this is it" said Simon finding it hard to believe they would be separated after spending so much time together.

One of the Chinese men was about to step forward and speak to Mai. Deng raised his hand and the man stopped and returned to his place. Mai turned around to face Simon. Suddenly she wrapped her arms around him in a gentle, loving embrace. She looked up at him and they kissed each other briefly with passion.

"You come back Simon understand?" she said sternly as she fought to hold back her emotion.

Simon simply smiled that cocky grin that for some reason was as reassuring as it was annoying. "Mai, don't worry because no matter what happens, we'll always have Dubai."

She hugged him tightly as if to say goodbye one more time. She broke away and entered the helicopter. Once she was inside the helicopter the four men got inside. Simon and the others backed away as the rotors began to spin faster and faster. As the helicopter began to rise, Simon could see Mai looking out the window at him.

He made a thumbs-up with his left hand and smiled at her, Mai repeated the gesture. The helicopter turned around and flew away toward the airport. Simon watched as it disappeared into the horizon. When the helicopter was gone, Simon turned around to face Deng and his team. "Ready to get down to business?" asked Simon.

Mack and Siobhan smiled eagerly. "Absolutely," they replied.

"Then let's get down to business," said Simon.

They shrugged their shoulders and walked back down the stairs. Before he walked down the stairs, he looked out at the sky and wondered if he would ever see Mai again. He also thought of Sheila. He shrugged and walked back down the stairs closing the door behind him.

The battle against the Networc continues in Book six of the Shadow World series: Never Say Forever…

About the Author

Robert Fisher was born in Long Branch, New Jersey. While attending Indian River State College in Florida, he began writing as a hobby that quickly turned into a passion for storytelling. After graduating from college, he sought to have his work published. He can be contacted on Facebook and Twitter at @ShadowWorld19. No One Lives Forever is his fifth book. If you enjoyed it, get ready, because the best is yet to come.....

Other Books by Robert Fisher

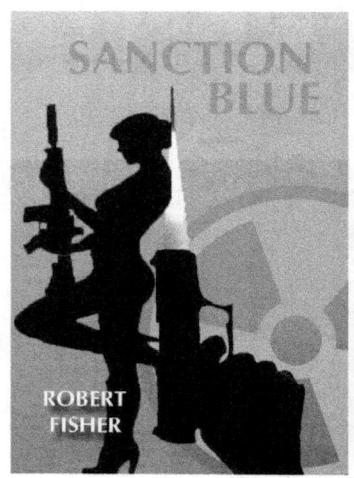

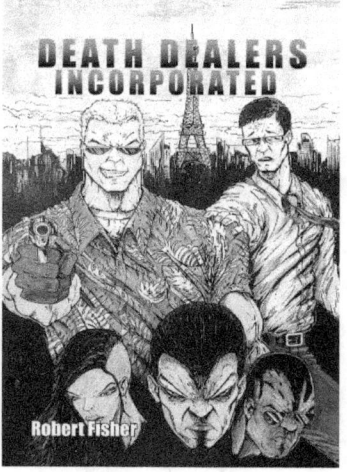

www.ingramcontent.com/pod-product-compliance
Lightning Source LLC
Chambersburg PA
CBHW070446260626
47161CB00004B/1219